GISÈLE VILLENEUVE

Rising Abruptly

STORIES

THE UNIVERSITY OF ALBERTA PRESS

Published by

The University of Alberta Press
Ring House 2
Edmonton, Alberta, Canada T6G 2E1
www.uap.ualberta.ca

Copyright © 2016 Gisèle Villeneuve

LIBRARY AND ARCHIVES CANADA
CATALOGUING IN PUBLICATION

Villeneuve, Gisèle, 1950-, author
    Rising abruptly : stories /
Gisèle Villeneuve.

(Robert Kroetsch series)
Issued in print and electronic formats.
ISBN 978-1-77212-261-9 (paperback).—
ISBN 978-1-77212-281-7 (EPUB).—
ISBN 978-1-77212-282-4 (mobipocket).—
ISBN 978-1-77212-283-1 (PDF)

    I. Title. II. Series: Robert Kroetsch
series

PS8593.I415R57 2016   C813'.54
C2016-901630-7
C2016-901631-5

First edition, first printing, 2016.
First printed and bound in Canada by
Houghton Boston Printers, Saskatoon,
Saskatchewan.
Copyediting and proofreading by
Maya Fowler-Sutherland.

A volume in the Robert Kroetsch Series.

The University of Alberta Press is
committed to protecting our natural
environment. As part of our efforts,
this book is printed on Enviro Paper: it
contains 100% post-consumer recycled
fibres and is acid- and chlorine-free.

The University of Alberta Press
gratefully acknowledges the support
received for its publishing program
from the Government of Canada, the
Canada Council for the Arts, and the
Government of Alberta through the
Alberta Media Fund.

Canada   Canada Council   Conseil des Arts
          for the Arts   du Canada

Albertan
Government

For Tom Back,
my partner in life and in the mountains,
always.

MOUNTAIN

A natural elevation of the earth's surface rising more or less abruptly from the surrounding level, and attaining an altitude which, relatively to adjacent elevations, is impressive or notable.

—*The Compact Edition of the Oxford English Dictionary*

Contents

1   Nuit Blanche with Gendarme

15   Jagged Little Peak

27   Benighted on Mighty Mount Royal

49   Kinabalu Realm of the Cold

91   Onion

131   Nepal High

151   Assiniboine Crossroads

199   *Acknowledgements*

Nuit Blanche with Gendarme

MY SISTER, a whirlwind inside my Calgary apartment. My sister taking me by storm. I prefer storms to stay outside. And I love my sister despite... Here she is. In my yellow kitchen. Arms scratched, fingernails broken, knuckles raw. And in her khaki shorts, legs black and blue.

What the hell happened to you? Come, sit down.

She won't sit. Stares at me with eyes so wild. So very wild. The dark eyes of Medea after she dispatched her children to the other world.

My sister says: It's because of my night with the gendarme.

Gendarme?

My sister has no children to drown in bathtubs or to strangle in the night and she is not given to having trouble with the law. I stare at her bruised legs. I keep my gaze there, because I simply cannot look at her burning eyes.

Gendarme, Sis? What gendarme?

We're in Calgary, not Paris. There are no gendarmes operating in this city. Why would she use that term?

What gendarme? Talk to me.

She asks for water. Her voice calm as a morning lake despite the storm that must be raging in her body. And I must resist looking at her eyes. So primal and wild, her Medea eyes.

She says: I'm thirsty, my dear brother. I can't tell you how perfectly thirsty I am.

I run the tap. Present her with a tall glass of cool water. She drinks and drinks and drinks. Such ecstasy over tap water. I'm a voyeur in spite of myself. Witnessing something unnamed. Can't begin to imagine her night at the hands of that gendarme. A visiting Frenchman? An exchange program with our city police? Maybe she met him in a bar after his shift. What did he trigger in her?

After quenching her thirst, if she has quenched it at all, my agitated sister paces up and down the kitchen. Gets set to tell me her story. Don't want to hear it. Yet, I must. I swallow hard, and the storm is unleashed.

▲ That day, an impulse leads her to the mountains.

Mountains?

Instead of driving to Banff like everyone else, and where we had been just days before, she veers off toward Kananaskis.

▲ Kananaskis, a region she could not possibly know. She, who not only has never expressed the slightest interest in orography, but, more importantly, has been scoffing at mountains ever since arriving in Calgary a few days ago, can't explain what brought her there.

Yes, yes, Sis, that's all very well, but, please, stay focused. What about the gendarme?

One mountain in particular draws her attention. Fascinates her. Galvanizes her into action. The attraction of one single mountain in a jumble of mountains, the same way that one man in a crowd would stand out for her alone.

She says: Believe it or not, I didn't believe it myself, but it hit me hard. What I felt was nothing short of a lightning strike of the heart.

That's it. The encounter in the bar. The one-night stand. She was using the parable of mountains to soften the blow. A lightning strike of the heart? Trust me. My skeptic sister is not given to love at first sight. Certainly not to long-term commitment.

She says: I was contemplating that mountain and, tout de suite, I *knew*. I *knew* I needed the vertical line not to fall. I *knew* the vertical line was the place to quiet your mind. There, in the silence among stones, I *knew*, I simply *knew* that I would find peace of mind at last. Please, more water.

I set a pitcher on the table. I sit down, she stands. And resumes pacing up and down the kitchen. She may seek a quiet mind, but her body will not relinquish frenzy. She drinks and can't quench her thirst.

Watching her, I try to understand without truly grasping what she is telling me. Ever since she was a little girl, she has been queen of the malcontents. Annoyed at everybody and anybody. Bristling with irritation, as if she did not belong in her own skin and had to shed it. Tonight, is she shedding? Sloughing off, to emerge as what? All her life, she has been a wanderer, running away from the noises and vexations of the world. Craving for, and failing to find, her elusive quiet centre.

I've had lots of time to think things through. I might as well tell you I've thought of precious little else, and, in stages, I developed a theory. First, I realized that, when she saw her mountain, my troubled sister identified a deeply rooted malaise. Later, it seemed, she discovered she was suffering from genuine vertigo on flat ground. What I ended up understanding most of all is that my disoriented sister *belongs* in the Rockies.

Elated, scratched, black and blue, she goes on: The search is over, brother. I've found myself at last. That's what I discovered during my night with the gendarme.

I look at her hard. Take the glass from her. Forbid her to drink until she tells me the true story, no matter how painful.

Gendarme, Sis. What goddam gendarme?

Relax and listen.

In a trance, she starts to climb her mountain.

I say: And you want *me* to *relax*? Look at you! You're a mess. You're shaking all over. And now you're telling me that you started climbing a *real* mountain? Just like that? What the hell's the matter with you? You have zero climbing experience. Nothing.

She says: Nothing but an instinct, nothing but an internal compass.

Standing in the middle of my kitchen, she re-enacts her moves.

▲ For hours, she scrambles up the scree.

Knees bent, she walks awkwardly along the kitchen floor. She hasn't yet learned to estimate elevation gain. She may be three hundred, perhaps six hundred metres above the valley. She can't say. She climbs on chairs, shields her eyes. Scrutinizes the floor.

So high up is she, and because of the broader perspective, cars appear as slowly moving toys along the road. So high up is she, their annoying car noises no longer reach her.

She says: Bliss. Blissful silence.

Now she climbs a jagged ridge. She is standing on the stove.

Exposure tugging at her back, she grips the rough limestone that abrades arms, cuts fingers, tumefies knuckles, shreds knees.

She paws cupboard doors. Reaches for knobs and hinges. Six hundred metres above ground (she figures), she hangs on, wrapping her arms around the hood of the fan above the stove. *Confident.* She is that confident, as if, with every move, the rock itself were teaching her how to climb. She runs the palms of her hands up the greasy wall near the ceiling. And, over there, she tells me, she was moving up her vertical line of rock with as much ease as me walking across my kitchen floor.

She tiptoes along the edge of the counter. The summit ridge becomes so narrow that my delicate sister must climb à cheval, a technique that consists of straddling the ridge, feet dangling over the void. She squats, dangling one leg off the counter and resting the other foot in the sink.

Only to imagine her in that terrifying position, not ninety-two centimetres off the kitchen floor, but six hundred metres above the valley floor, my heart climbs into my mouth and my ears start to buzz. I am overtaken by *real* vertigo.

I feel the wind as she jumps off the counter to rush to my rescue.

Curled up on the floor, I scream at her: You could have killed yourself. Are you raving mad?

She spins across the tiles, chanting: Madly in love, oh, yeah. So very, very madly in love. And it is for life, my dear brother. *For life.* Get up.

Now, I know something is very wrong. I pick myself up. Pick up my chair. Sit down, head in hands. For life, I repeat in my head. For life, I repeat in my hands. For life.

At long last, we get to the goddam gendarme. Honestly, I had forgotten about the rotten man. Man! I go straight from debilitating vertigo to jittery laughter. Can't stop sputtering wise cracks. Now, it is my puzzled sister's turn to think that I am the mad one. Not mad. Relieved. I pour her a fresh glass of water. Watch her drink.

I say: Let me guess. You met an experienced climber, right? A partner who kept you from falling. And one thing leading to the next, your night with that gendarme. Now, I understand. What a relief! A liaison—tightly tied to your lover's climbing rope, I hope—a liaison on a mountain isn't cozy as in a great big bed or soft as a roll in the hay, right? A night of lovemaking on rock is bound to leave scrapes and bruises. Isn't that right, eh, Sis?

I laugh and laugh, relieved. Dear me! So very much relieved.

▲ You see, more and more Europeans flock to our Rockies, because their Alps are crawling with crowds lining up to climb. So, on her mountain, my sister met a Frenchman. Nothing unusual. After all, it was a Frenchman, Doctor Michel-Gabriel Paccard, who invented mountain climbing. And way back in 1786. Almost exactly three years before his countrymen took the Bastille by storm. As for Paccard, he took Mont Blanc by grit and gall on August 8th, 1786. Accompanied by a resident of Chamonix, the hunter Jacques Balmat. Yes, I know these mountain-related things. Possibly because I am overly attached to flat ground, I very much enjoy reading about people who choose to give themselves trouble, sometimes impossibly great trouble, clinging to rock. So, it is conceivable that my ethereal sister met a climber who happens to be a French gendarme on holiday in our Rockies.

I ask: Is he a Jacques Balmat, of the rough-and-tumble hunter type, or a Paccard, of the considerate country doctor type?

Now, it is my sister's turn to laugh: The things you dream up, brother! A gendarme is a rock tower occupying and blocking an arête.

Of course, I know that in mountain parlance, a gendarme is a rock tower occupying and blocking an arête. But how does she know that? I must tell you the day after she landed in Calgary to visit me, although heights make me truly queasy, I dutifully brought my grumbling sister to Banff and Lake Louise to see the mountains. She barely glanced at them, declaring that she shared painter Alex Colville's opinion that mountains are silly. So, you can imagine my dismay that evening when she storms into my kitchen, gushing about the gendarme, silence among stones and quiet mind on the vertical line. More to the point though, that evening, I so wish a man with climbing experience, French or not, and not too audacious, were with her to keep her safe. I so wish she were not alone with her mountain. Any *silly* mountain.

Seriously, I ask: A gendarme, eh? How big was your gendarme, the one blocking the way?

Taller than a tall man.

You can't climb on. Can you downclimb?

I didn't get that far only to bail at the first obstacle.

What did you do then? With your gendarme taller than a tall man? Standing on the edge of the precipice?

My metamorphosing sister keeps quiet for a long time. She and I in growing darkness, in deepening silence. I sit, she stands. Both of us quiet. For a long time.

She pours herself a glass of water. Drinks. Climbs on the end of the counter.

She says: In fading light, I can see that, farther on, the ridge is rising abruptly. To continue, I'll have to wait until morning. But something tells me that I must contour the gendarme before sunset. You see, this is a rite of passage. If I ace that test, tomorrow I'll reach the summit.

Rite of passage?

The motor of the fridge kicks in.

How did you manage that?

It was a rather intimate encounter with the gendarme.

In other circumstances, I'd fall back on dumb locker-room jokes. Not tonight. No. In the darkness filling my kitchen, darkness falling on the rocky ridge where my addle-brained sister is perched, I am too moved to laugh, too petrified to move. An initiation into the mysteries of what she calls the vertical line. This can't be my sister the unbeliever talking. And yet, here she is, standing on the end of the kitchen counter, talking about rite of passage, initiation, falling in love. Where might that lead, if not to disaster, certainly to another disappointment?

My usually sharp-tongued, impatient sister speaks softly. In a voice I never knew she had. A voice to share secrets. I am listening. Holding my breath. Even Calgary outside my kitchen window, I swear, is holding its breath. So silent the summer evening, it may have drifted into town from a very ancient place. Oh! To capture such rare silence and offer it to my strange sister, so that she would agree to stay among us, flatlanders.

My zany sister, who has no experience, no gear, no partner— my sister, whom I love dearly, is, to go around the gendarme, about to face deadly exposure.

She demonstrates. Wraps her arms around her gendarme. She hugs the fridge. Stretches her left leg and, on the side of the drop, finds a tiny hold on which to rest her big toe. She stretches her leg as far as it will go across the fridge to reach the other section of the counter. Her stance looks unstable. She'll fall. To reach the other side of the ridge, she must jump.

She says: Just a short jump.

Jump? Jump? Are you crazy? Jump as in *jump*?

My heart skips a beat. A *short* jump! How short is short? What else is she required to do? Perform a swan dive? The leap of death?

Deadly calm, hugging the fridge, my lunatic sister gets on with her story: I must do that little hop to free the tiny hold on which my left big toe is resting and make room for the tip of my right foot. You understand, there's not much room for error...

At this cliffhanger, I hit *pause*, interrupting the flow of the narrative, to make an observation that has probably occurred to you already. My charming sister is standing in my kitchen, in an off-balance position on the edge of the counter, telling me about her night with her gendarme, so it is obvious that she survived her one-night stand with the mountain. Also, as I mentioned earlier, although I am a man who enjoys his routine in a safe and familiar environment, I get my thrill vicariously by reading accounts similar to the one unfolding tonight in my kitchen. Even if those accounts are written in the first person *after the fact*, making it clear that the author survived the ordeal, as I turn the pages, I allow myself a certain measure of emotional involvement, suspending my disbelief and playing along. As I am doing this evening. With the exception that, in this case, I care a whole lot more about the narrator of this tale than I do about any writer-adventurer whom I will never personally know. So, tonight, I greatly fear the future. After all, my emotional sister is in the grip of first love. And gravity, maw wide-opened, awaits. I hit *play*. Let's get this narrative over with.

...There's not much room for error. With my left foot, I feel my way to safety along the flat ridge on the other side of the gendarme.

I shout: Safety? What safety is there in hopping over the void?

She stretches and rests the tip of her big toe on the section of the counter beyond the fridge. Pushing with her other leg and gripping the sides of the polished, cold white fridge, she lunges. And loses her footing.

I jump up from my chair, try to break her fall and, together, we tumble to the floor. I holler. She laughs.

She says: Obviously, up there, it went without a hitch.

At this point, I'm so bewildered, I slap and hug her at the same time.

I yell: The mountain has gone to your head. Snap out of it. Right this minute, snap out of this. Neither of us has ever been a big supporter of love at first sight. What your climbing Frenchman, if he existed at all, would call the coup de foudre.

She says, giddy and raising a finger: But, dear brother, that's *exactly* what it is.

I continue, still yelling: This insane situation proves the point. Besides, must I remind you that, a few days ago, you declared mountains to be silly? When are you planning to go back home? Away from this delusion? When?

She laughs. Picks herself off the floor. Reaches for the pitcher of water. Drinks in big gulps. Lets it drip off her chin.

She says: I hug my gendarme with all my might. We are very intimate. As the sun's going down, I am making love to an entire mountain. And think what you will. It is *not* silly.

I sit down squarely on my chair. And say: Suddenly, *not* silly, the mountains?

She is beyond rational thought. If my usually cynical sister's uncharacteristic behaviour tonight is not the result of *silly* love at first sight, it's possible that she is suffering from a mild form of mountain sickness. Altitude sickness, that is real enough. Disorientation. Brain edema. If you don't come down to a lower altitude, death. Granted. The mountains in Kananaskis Country are not high enough to cause altitude sickness, but my lovely sister is a lowland creature. Who's to know if even the mild elevation in Calgary isn't affecting her. Beside myself with endless speculations, I can't stop fidgeting on my chair. Can't control the palpitations. Black dots pulsate in front of my eyes. Any second, I'll drop dead in my kitchen filled with darkness and secrets, while the wretched gendarme remains stone cold in the face of this dizzy affair. Saying dizzy affair may convey aloofness on my part. Trust me. I was, am, anything but detached.

Out there, up there, daylight dims. The land loses its relief. My elated sister has a trickle of a pee before she ties herself to the gendarme until dawn. With what? Since she has no climbing rope, what does she use to secure herself to the mountain? Her long hair? I don't dare ask.

This, I ask: The night must have been endless? Dark? You must have been thirsty? Cold? You must have been in pain? Afraid?

The yellow walls of my kitchen have lost their cheerfulness. I keep seeing my sister storming in, limbs black and blue. And her wild, wild eyes that will always haunt me. And that urgency of hers: gimme water.

She answers my questions: You know how impatient I am. I thought dawn would never come. How wrong I was! Au contraire. Night flies. Don't you see? Already, I am honing patience on the rock. Did you know? Stones multiply at night. It must be so, because the more broken rocks I removed from under me, the more there were. And the night. How extraordinary, the night! Even without moonlight it was never dark, because the sky was a riot of stars. Maybe not very comfortable, reclining on stones, but no tossing and turning, no fidgety mind. Simply, dear brother, simply, stillness.

In my kitchen, my over-the-moon-in-love sister drinks. Paces and drinks. Won't she sit down? She won't sit down. And that thirst that cannot be quenched.

Oh, yes, up there throughout the night, thirst torments her. In the starlight, her gendarme invites her to lick its stone. A trickle of moisture seeping through limestone. Moisture that, during the day, the sun evaporates instantly. But at night, the limestone releases water, an offering. The trickle appeases her thirst a little. Never fully.

The wind rises. A devilish wind bent on pushing her into the void. Now, she's freezing on her pile of rock. Unsheltered, she shivers.

She says: My gendarme whispers in the wind. I get closer. And would you believe it? The rock feels warmer, very much warmer, as if it were in direct sunlight.

I say: Whispers? You mean, you hear the wind whistling against the stone formation?

She says: My gendarme, hard and cold, turns out to be warm and tender. The ideal lover.

On my chair, I shiver, too overcome with profound inquiétude to respond.

What now? Rats are moving in on her. Packrats. Where are they coming from? She can't say. Those rodents of the heights gnaw away at climbing ropes, but my sister has no gear of any kind. And so, she claims, the wind and the packrats become the messengers of the mountain. Overnight, she learns everything there is to learn about climbing.

Her monolithic gendarme tells her mountain tales. He moans the names of all the mountains for the climbing. She repeats the names to remember them. The litany lasts all night. He whistles those secrets deep into her bones and sinews, heart and mind. She engraves the secrets deep into her memory. As rocks multiply on her hard bed, her stone lover seduces my limber sister with mountain science, with mountain lore.

I can't resist cautioning her: My dear little sister, beware. People put a great deal of meaning, too big a deal, in stories of stones.

She says: I was never good at love. How to make a guy happy. How to understand his silences. How to laugh with him and not at him. How not to lose patience each time he drops crumbs on the floor.

So, that's it. To escape a life spent sweeping floors, my inflexible sister falls in love with a limestone gendarme; my passionate sister falls in love with the vertical line. That's what she calls the seduction of wild land. The wild, always the same, and yet, always changing, like an attentive and inventive lover.

It is my turn to whisper: And fear? How do you deal with it?

She says: Fear is as strong as the void that tugs at you. It's a little blue flame that dances on the rock beside you. Vertigo gnaws away at your resolve the same way that time works on a fortress that lasted one thousand years and collapses it in one second. But up there, you don't think about vertigo. You don't think about the fall. Your entire being is utter focus. Up there, you are no longer distracted. All of your concentration dances on a needle.

Again I whisper: And bloody skin, Angel? Surely, your torn flesh?

She says: Your body no longer exists. You have no skin, no bladder, no stomach. Even your thirst, you ignore. All your pain centres are closed for the day. And you climb. Up there, your body works for you. How to explain? Your body in action works for you, but also, it carries you outside of itself. Love? The sublime? Words fail, dear brother. Words fall off. You no longer need words. All I can tell you right now is that you know, *you know*, that you'll do anything to stay in that state. What you will give up, how far you will go to be in that silence, to remain in that frame of mind. In the quiet. It is the most joyous vertical gymnastics you could ever imagine. A slow, slow dance with an entire mountain.

▲ And tonight, in my kitchen, now black as a pot, I am dizzy with vertigo, numb with mixed emotions. I still hear my mysterious sister's whispers: Holding on to my vertical line, I am up there for life. Holding on to my vertical line, I am in love with a stone gendarme who will keep sharing his secrets with me forever.

In my kitchen black as a pot, even though she left a long time ago, I hear my tragic sister breathing. I see her silhouette dancing on chairs. Walking across the counter. Hugging the ghostly white shape of the fridge. Even though it has been so long, I see her shadow-shape. And every evening, I refill the pitcher with cold, clear water. Her glass on the table still marked with her fingerprints, the rim still bearing the imprint of her lips. And every evening, the pitcher, her glass and I, we are waiting for her to storm in here with the full brunt of her wildness. Even though I know that *that* evening, she whirlwinded into here to say her farewells to me. To say her farewells to the safe and the familiar.

That was five years ago.

I will never overcome my fear of heights. But you, if you go into the Rockies, if you feel the seduction of wild land, if you hear the wind sing between stones, perhaps it is my sister, with her will steady as a rock, talking to you. She may be an entire mountain. Be kind to her wildness.

And when you come back down to my flat ground, I would dearly love if you stopped by and told me how she is.

Jagged Little Peak

MY HANDS RAW from the scrape of stone. My daughter's hands caked with blood. Not yet seventeen and she sneaks back home at dawn with bloody hands. I search the smooth limestone face. Insert my left fingers into a thin fracture. Cup a nodule jutting from the solid mass with my right fingers and wedge my toes into narrow cracks. I haul myself up another metre. Repeat the moves over and over.

Wind whistles in my helmet and rough stone tears into my fingertips. I reach a slanting ledge covered with rubble. To avoid the risk of an eight-hundred-metre fall to the valley floor, I wrap nylon slings around a couple of rock horns and clip in another sling girth-hitched to my harness. Safely anchored to the mountain, I throw up with abandon.

A raven perches on an exposed ridge, showing interest in the disgorged matter. Its croaking echoes my daughter's sniggering words.

Mom, you're such a chicken.

In a glint of sun, the bird's feathers are bleached. My Alex, white face carved in snow, hands etched in scarlet. Alexandra dances barefoot on serrated stone. Sniffs the wind and throws herself over the edge, her long black hair floating behind her.

Another glint of sun, and the raven folds its wings and dives into the abyss. Dizzy, I grab the stone.

A rock slide tumbles between two ribs of the mountain. I listen to the hollow sound of rocky debris shattering as the stones bounce high before landing far below. For a long time, I hear them collide into their resting place. At dawn, our daughter triggered her own rock slide.

I just told you, Mom. I had a fight with Jan. I am not staying at her house. No way.

Come with us. You used to love climbing.

She accused me again. Me and these stupid mountains. Me and my stupid obsession. She hates everything and everything is stupid. Most of all, she hates to comply.

Sam stepped over the rocks of hatred strewn about our kitchen.

Sweetheart, today is your Mom's fortieth birthday.

Alex hung her head, tears welling in her mascara-smeared eyes.

This is a special climb for us. You know. Our jagged little peak, he finished with a disarming smile.

Alex sank to the floor. Sam held me in his arms.

Jo, we can't leave.

Can't you see? She's playing you against me.

There's a serious problem, here. We have to deal with it. What's going on?

Tethered to my ledge, I urge him to read her diary. He knows it doesn't count as snooping. Peering at the void, I mumble: At least, let it be her own blood. In the kitchen, Sam whispered to me that the mountain could wait, then gently put his hand on top of mine. Now, something soft brushes across my wrist. Startled, I slip on the rubble. Would have gone over the edge, but for the grace of my slings tying me to the mountain. Sam whispers in my throbbing ear that you don't climb in anger.

I'm forty, love, I tell the rocks. I couldn't wait. I wouldn't wait.

Sam chose to stay home. I had no choice but to climb alone. For a whole week, fighting dread and nausea, I had psyched myself up to such a degree, I couldn't let go of the anticipation. At last, today we would succeed, we would stand on the summit. Three times in two years, we've had to turn back. Hail and verglas. Then, danger of avalanche when we ventured out too early in the season. And last time, my slip. The fall left me too freaked to climb on, and with slashes across my arms that would not heal. And this morning, Alex's eyes dared me to climb solo. She dared me. I had no choice.

The raven glides above my ledge. Better get moving before you turn to stone. Go ahead. Holler. It'll help shake off your inertia and dismiss the irrational fear that has made you sick for a quarter century. I scrutinize the waves of rock walls and ribs and chimneys guarding the summit. This is as far as Sam and I managed to climb. From here on, I am on new ground. Must push upward, alone. On this day of my fortieth, the cloudless sky heartens me.

Grip the rock, raise one foot, heave yourself a little higher with each thrust of the body. Let hands and feet find cracks, let flesh and rock mesh, let no thought enter the mind. Establish the rhythm of the climb and the mountain may grant a moment of happiness. The afternoon spins fast on its axis, time unnoticed, body and mind so utterly engaged.

Sprawling shadows force me to look at the sky. Holy scree! Thunderheads. I reach a shallow alcove between vertical ribs.

Lightning. Pinned in my narrow niche, I expect the next thunderbolt to crucify me, to turn me into a carbonized casualty of the summer climbing season. Alex and the lightning strobes of her diary.

Jan begging me to go to that party. Would be cool, she said. It was—the beer, the guitars. Until that dude showed up with his old

man's rifle. Idiot, full of pride and power. Then the shot went off.
Everybody scattering, screaming. Jan whimpering on the concrete
floor, coughing and shrieking. Begging me to get her out of there.
She's so dumb. I kicked that asshole in the jaw with my foot. A side
kick as I was lying on the floor. Kind of reminded me of splayed
legs on a rock climb. Stretching to reach a solid hold. Good move, I
thought. Good move! Mom and Dad would shout over the wind. The
guy dropped the gun, shaking all over. I grabbed Jan and ran out
with everybody in tow.

Ah, Alex. Lightning. Thunder. Recently, my daughter has been rewriting the book of risks. Two guys tailing her, she on foot, they in their pickup truck.

How does it feel to be scared? I could ask Mom. Had to find out
for myself. Running into an alley. The pickup engine screaming in the
dead of night. The guys swaggering out of their truck. Me, running
and running.

Alex, oh, Alex. Prey caught in the glare of headlights. Bolts of lightning criss-cross the black sky tinged with verdigris and leave the tingle of static electricity on my face. The storm rolls over me. At seventeen, I left the tamed nature of the east for the wild thrill of the west. I met Sam on the slopes, another crazy easterner bored with manicured lakefront cottages. We lost ourselves in the hills, learning the ropes, as it were, by trial and no error. Together, we discovered—we thought we invented—the way of the mountains.

Although as committed as Sam, on our way to every climb, I had to disappear among the last trees before we hit the rock. He teased me about my weak bladder and I managed to grin before throwing up on the moss. The vomiting ritual went on undetected for eight years until I became pregnant. Blaming morning sickness, I didn't have to hide anymore. Concerned for my health, he exhorted me to stop climbing. Nothing to do with

morning sickness, Sam. I had to disclose my shameful secret.
In the scree, I stood to lose it all. His love, his friendship, his
confidence in such a craven partner. To make me feel better,
or maybe he spoke the truth, he told me he knew all along.
To make me feel better, but now I know he spoke the truth,
he confessed to restlessness before every climb. That day, we
climbed superbly.

Rain turning to hail pelts me. Under the hood of my rain gear,
I huddle head between knees, closing myself off from the wild.
What kind of game my Alex played in the slick wild of the city
last night, I wonder. I blame myself for teaching her fearlessness.
Look, Mom! No hands. Hands smeared with blood, now. Crimson
across the sky. Thunder.

The storm moves on. I resume the climb, my mental battle
in full swing, the rock wet and slippery. The higher I climb, the
more I commit. The more I commit, the less willing I am to bail.
Exposure increases and, directly below, the patient stones await
to receive my fallen body. I repeat the solo climber's mantra:
You must not fall. You must not fall. Concentration, technique
and strength allow me a measure of bliss. Until the next crack
opens in my resolve. Anxiety dilates my pupils, making the world
blindingly bright. Slackens my muscles, now on fire. I growl and
it scurries away, though watchful, ready to pounce in a gust of
wind or when I reach and find nothing but rotten holds. After
the storm, my inner storm in full swing.

Endless waves of rock rise before me, hiding a summit that
may exist only in imagination. Lore has it that the mountain
reveals itself only when you stand on it. I cross one rib of rock
to climb an easier one. Soon realize my mistake, as the gully
steepens over even greater exposure. I have no choice but to
downclimb. I ain't no cat stuck in a tree. I can do this. Pushing
outward with my arms braced against the two opposing walls

of the gully, I inch my way down, my dangling feet searching the rock, my brain willing them to land on something. Before crossing back to the first rib, I rest in the safety of a small chimney, crouching among the broken limestone, arms bleeding.

I almost gave birth to you, Alex, in a similar chimney. To the eleventh hour, I climbed with you in my belly. And then, we had to race down to the hospital. A sight we looked, dirty and smelly after four days in the hills. The nurses removed my harness, clanking with gear, but I gave birth with my climbing boots on. To hell with hygiene, I remember shouting. That kid nearly popped out on the rocks. Besides, the boots would give me great traction. I demanded to rope up, anchored to pegs driven into the delivery room wall. Your father reassured the staff I wasn't as crazy as I sounded and, despite himself looking like Mr. Sasquatch, he helped me climb down from my frenzy. Still, I insisted: With my boots on!

I clip in to a couple of pitons on an exposed ledge where I will remain until dawn. Day turned to dusk before I could stand on my elusive summit. In the shadows at my feet, I notice embedded into the rock a metal cross bearing the name and age of a climber. He was so young when he died. Had he, at least, made it to the top, before the fall? I stare at the void. Hundreds of metres of air. I stare and stare until I feel nothing. Only then do I take off my pack, clip it to the pitons and phone Sam to let him know I won't be home tonight.

His demeanour is breezy, but even with the poor signal, I detect concern in his voice; the one at home always bears the brunt of the worry.

How's Alex?

She's fine. Cut her hands on some glass.

He tells me more, something about a contest and Cossack dancing, but we're about to lose the connection.

See you later tomorrow, Sam.

Say hello to our jagged little peak. And take care.

From my perch so high up, I watch the void fill with darkness and the surrounding rock lose its definition in the grainy greyness of dusk, while the sky above will remain full of light for hours. Alex's diary is like rock and evening sky. Darkness and brilliance.

So, Mom grounded me for sneaking out to the party of the year. She's been showing me how to survive ever since I was a kid. And now what? Pretending to be a typical mother. Understanding nothing. She's never been like that. And I'm no fool. I deserve her trust.

Ah, she did learn my survival lessons too well.

Look, Mom! No hands.

And I recall a page, crowded with silver stars she glued in the margins and around the last sentence.

Climbers don't stop climbing just because they have kids. They're hooked. One more fix. And it's that last fix...

The rough stone grinds into the small of my back. I shift position. When I try to talk to her, she slinks away. Sam fares better. From time to time, I find them sitting side by side on the back stairs, recalling climbing moments. She never lambastes him for keeping up his mountain pursuit. Alex, a mystery to me at the moment. Alex, wild, stubborn, but not a delinquent. An achiever in the classroom, she discovered early that if you do well in school, you could get away with eccentric behaviour. Even though she's popular, she spends hours alone behind closed doors. I leave her be.

I blame myself for setting her off on her dubious course. Cowardice, I swore, would never plague my daughter. She was five when we fitted her with a full-body climbing harness, and on her eighth birthday, we gave her her first mountaineering axe. She scampered up anything vertical with the surefootedness of a mountain goat. However proud of Alex's climbing abilities,

Sam reminded her that a healthy dose of fear separates the courageous from the foolhardy, preserves life and elevates the spirit. We argued the point while I crushed in her any manifestation of the bashful, the timorous, the pusillanimous. I'd have none of it. Wild land is not your enemy, Alex. Learn the climbing techniques well. Learn to assess risks. Wild nature became my daughter's second nature.

Six months ago, she gave up climbing and took up running.

The wild doesn't scare me one bit. Never has. Now, pitting myself against human violence. Anything more terrifying than that? Will I ever know, what she feels, my mother?

▲ Dawn. In spite of clinging to an exposed, impossibly smooth slab, but this being the crux, I am climbing with rare confidence. After the crux, one has only to scramble up on the easy summit ridge. I'll make it. I'll make it for Sam, for her. For all of us. But, oh, no...

The face retracts from under me. I fall. Not far. Maybe ten metres. I land hard on my back. Red flashes shoot across my eyes. I count on my pack to have softened the blow to my vertebrae. High above, the raven glides in morning light. The young dead climber whispers: Did you make the summit, at least? My daughter screams on the wind, her hands dripping with thick blood. At least, let it be her own. Don't let me read in her diary about a man with a knife, a struggle, Alex defending herself, the man lying on the ground, his throat cut. On the wind, I sniff the scent of dead animals; hear Alex's voice distorted by distance. Don't let me hear her say she tried to close the slit with her hands, begging for my help in stitching up the man's throat, she didn't mean to. My mind is swimming in and out of consciousness and I wish for my daughter the same sudden raw release of fear as with the young man brandishing his father's rifle at that party. The raven croaks. Leaves my field of vision.

I check the stone under my buttocks. Feel nothing, as if the impact had knocked the terror right out of me. I must get up. Reach that summit. I lie here, waiting. We must resume our tango danced a thousand times with high steps and careful dips over the void. I will dance with you again, Sam.

I unclip the cell from my harness. Dial in a daze. Will it connect? Last night, what did he tell me about her hands? Something about Cossacks and glass...

Alex?

Mom!

Your dad home?

He left early. Did you make it?

I hear a tremolo in her voice. I'd hoped Sam had not gone to work yet, the morning so young, so bright.

As calmly as possible, I explain. Listen to me, Alex. I'll try to rappel. It'll be slow. Once I'm down, I'll have the hike back to the car. It'll take all day.

Mom, I'm losing you.

The signal is weakening.

Mom, don't move. Do you hear? Stay where you are. They won't find you otherwise. Where are you? Describe it. Mom?

Now, finally, Sam's words filter through, the things he said yesterday. Some kids were having a bottle-smashing contest. Glass everywhere. Alex slipped and broke her fall with both hands flat on the ground. In the stance of a Cossack dancer. Broke her fall. I exhale, close my eyes. Her own blood on her hands. She is yelling in my ear.

Mom? Are you there?

Not going anywhere.

Mom? Mom?

You have a pen?

I describe where I fell. The signal is getting spotty. Gaps between our words.

Alex, I'm losing the connection.

Okay, I got it. Hang on. I know what to do.

Although the pain in my lower back is searing now, I'm reassured when I can move fingers and toes. Alex alone in the house. Will she phone the wardens' office right away? Try to reach her dad at work and let him take charge? Tears run down the side of my face.

Oh, Alex, to this day, I don't understand my distraction. Pregnant, I mean. I looked at my belly in disbelief the day I strained to buckle up my harness over you. The thing growing inside me that took control. I could no longer self-arrest. An internal rope tied us together, a rope that you would cut only at the time of impact. You birthed yourself, a puzzle that had nothing to do with me. Sam, on this clear, clear morning, you, so intimately tied to me, seem all of a sudden too far to reach. I'm thirsty. At an incredible distance from my head, I glimpse my feet shod in scuffed boots.

Boots! So that's what made me peel off. I think back to last night, switching from rock shoes to hiking boots for warmth and comfort. And this morning, forgot to switch back again. Holy scree! How distracted am I?

I can only laugh. The nurses assumed it was maternal happiness that made me giggly. It wasn't that. It was thinking I had just given birth to twin cracked-leather boots. Staring at my feet through tears of mirth, failing to understand how I could have been allowed to deliver a child, in a hospital, with my boots on, I formed the notion that I had, at last, expelled my congenital fear.

Not so. It had never left me. This morning acknowledging my distraction, it's all too clear. Forever, I'll climb, fall and climb again, pushing before me the rock of my dread. If there is one consolation, it is that, in the delivery room, I didn't pass that damn emotion on to my daughter. My only wish now is for her to stop trying so hard to experience it. Staring at the sky, I imagine Sam up on the ridge above, egging me on, both of us clinging to our jagged little peak, and, despite the sharp pain across my ribs forcing me to shallow my breathing, I can't stop laughing. Here I come, love. Here I come.

I swallow dryness, my tears distorting Sam's face and the light.

Benighted / on Mighty Mount Royal

AS IF RACHEL WANTED to go tobogganing. The cold, the snow. Her father died in the cold in the snow. In those distant mountains. The wool sweaters that make you itchy. The tuque that makes you look ugly. The mitts that make you clumsy. His tuque and mitts and itchy sweaters did not keep him from turning into a snowman. The slushy streets, the boots always damp. Damp. As if Rachel wanted to go tobogganing.

But the game, Rachel! We must play the game.

Yes, Jeanne. The game.

Rachel understands that she and her cousin must play the sacred game. And this afternoon, Jeanne wants to go tobogganing, so that they can play the game. And when Jeanne wants something...

Don't worry so much, Rach. On Mount Royal, the snow will be friendly. Nothing like the snow on those giant mountains. So very far away. Jeanne also reminds her cousin that, once back home, Rachel always says she loved the game. The *aftermath*, the power.

The aftermath. A word Rachel's mom had taught the cousins. Sounds like after the math. Homework done, problem solved. The reward, out of the cold, safe from the snow, Rachel slurping a hot chocolate, her feet toasty in her slippers. Rachel dissecting the game. One thing she loves above all else is dissecting. In the coziness of aftermath, she keeps adding to the game events of epic proportion. So as usual, she yields to Jeanne's persuasion.

When they reach the foot of Mount Royal, the December afternoon is already drawing to a close, the temperature dropping quickly, and forecasting a frigid night. In the fading light of day, Jeanne notices dark clouds forming over the mountain.

Her mouth hidden behind her wool scarf, she curses her cousin and her crazy ideas: Let's go home, Jeanne. Before my toes turn into hard candies.

Come on, Rach, don't be a crybaby. We're eleven. Not two. Make yourself tough. You'll see. When we start sliding, we'll warm up and you'll love it. Let's run to the bus stop.

Pulling the toboggan, they run against the wind. The sharp air brings tears to their eyes. Under their feet, the snow cracks like caramelized sugar. With each breath, their nostrils stick together and the glacial air pinches their lungs. At the bus stop, they stamp their feet, endure the cold knocking on their foreheads. And the bus fails to appear. Jeanne suggests that they play the game of hiking the trail that climbs to the summit. Soon, the paved road that parallels the trail disappears behind fir trees loaded with snow. Between the trees, the cousins glimpse several buses driving back to the city.

Jeanne climbs the trail with much energy. Rachel follows more slowly, pulling the toboggan tied to its red cord. In the snow between the stems of the naked shrubs, sparrows' tracks have left exclamation marks.

Jeanne waits for her cousin: Come on, Rach. My turn to pull the toboggan.

No, no. I can do this. Walk!

They resume the hike, watching the city lights below, a scene straight out of a Christmas card. 'Tis the twelfth month, Christmas is very much on their minds.

When they reach the lake, not quite at the summit, Jeanne looks around: Eh, Rach! See that? The place's deserted. Where's everybody?

That's right. The snowy slopes have been abandoned. On frozen lac des Castors, not one soul is skating. And, out of the loudspeakers, not one note of a waltz streams into the cold air. The girls don't understand this anomaly, since in the glittery season, the place crawls with winter-loving people, even on weeknights. The parking lot lies empty and the windows of the lodge are dark.

Rachel feels all funny inside, disoriented and uneasy. As if a giant hand had dropped her in a strange land.

Let's go back down, Jeanne. I'm really, really cold.

Oh, Rach, this is great! How often do we get to have the entire mountain to ourselves!

Jeanne's right. A tiny part of Rachel wants this adventure. But how she wishes it was already over. How she wishes she was back home, dissecting. Still pulling the narrow sled, which seems heavier now, she follows her cousin, leading the way toward the summit.

Jeanne searches for the deepest powder, the girls sinking in up to their knees. Giggling, Jeanne kneels on the toboggan and remains afloat: Look, Rach! Like a magic carpet!

Catching the thrill, a little, Rachel also kneels on the magic carpet. Then, the girls stand up, pretending to surf like those boys in the Hawaiian TV show. Only, they lose their balance and fall into the snow as into the sea. Sharks! they shriek. Still in the shelter of the fir trees, they make snow angels before trudging toward a fallen log to catch their breath. They look up. Spot one star. Fancy it is the Star of Bethlehem.

With one whip of wind, clouds pack into the parcel of sky visible above the trail. The star vanishes. Raving through the trail, the wind throws bullet-hard snow pellets at the girls' faces. The blast latches on their mouths, stifling breath. To draw air, they must turn their backs to the wind. Around them, the treetops now swing wildly, their trunks creaking.

Jeanne, this is omin... This is not good!

To be heard in this hurricane, Jeanne has to shout: You're right. Let's go back down.

Unlike Jeanne that, to agree so quickly. Which should have sounded an alarm. But doesn't. Instead, Rachel sees herself back home in one hour. Tops. The cold makes her want to pee, but hating public toilets, and hating even more to pee in the open, she will hold the flow. Once home, she will rush into the privacy of the warm bathroom to relieve her bloated bladder. Sighing with pleasure, she will dissect the hike in cold and snow, the challenge, taken up and won.

The girls walk, heads dunked into coat collars, eyes fixed on their boots, as if the footwear could show them the way. No longer a shelter, the trail has transformed into a wind tunnel filled with a wall of snow. Red dots dance in front of their eyes and they can no longer see the firs that, up to now, guarded their adventure.

Rachel bumps into a tree hidden in the whiteness. Stunned, she collapses, calls out to Jeanne, but the wind eats her words before they reach her cousin's ears. Jeanne disappears from view. That's it. Rachel will die here, as her father died in those faraway mountains. She whimpers and crawls on the toboggan as on her deathbed: Father! I'm coming up! And so, already deep into playing the game of her death, it takes her a moment before she feels Jeanne's red face against her own. Lightheaded, she loses her balance.

Jeanne helps her cousin to her feet: I'll pull the sled now.

No! It's my toboggan. I'm okay. Rachel touches the hurt on her forehead. Blood, like red gelatin, sticks to her mitt: I'm dizzy. We'll die.

We're not gonna die.

We will too.

Okay, Rach, die if you want. But first, tie one end of my scarf around your waist and I'll tie the other end around my waist.

Instead of reassuring her, this precaution intensifies Rachel's fear. This is how people die in mountain stories. Tied to each other. And so will they, under tons of snow, a bit of red scarf sticking out to mark their glacial grave. But walk they must.

And so, nearly blinded by the storm, Rachel keeps moving, step by step, her face offered to gusts of wind, her neck touched by the thousand frozen fingers of snow. Only the tension of the scarf around her waist, which pulls her forward when Jeanne walks a little faster, proves that the cousins are linked together. Despite that tether, Rachel imagines herself lost and alone in wild mountains on the other side of the world.

Trees have become cliffs between which she is climbing a hair's breadth from dizzying exposure. She must progress with great caution. Over snow bridges that could collapse into deep valleys. Through avalanche terrain where wind has deposited deadly snow. Under seracs hanging above her head. Her limbs have turned to wood and her body is bruised with cold and exhaustion. Famished and tormented by thirst, she trips in her numb feet. Her hard candy toes that, surely, will have to be amputated. She hates Jeanne for turning the sacred game into a disaster. But, even if the toboggan was a true magic carpet capable of flying her home in an instant, she cannot call off the game. She and her cousin must conquer the virgin mountain. Must succeed in this rescue mission in the frozen hell. Together, they search the Himalayas, away from all humans and all beasts. At this high altitude against the deserted flank of the goddess mountain, mistress of vast blue spaces, and of death, even the eagle never glides. Somewhere among the folds and the crevasses, the crags and the ledges, her father and her aunt are dying. Courage! Hang on! Rachel and Jeanne will plead with the goddess mountain. Together, the cousins will rescue their parents. Having learned about the madness triggered by thin air, Rachel allows herself a brief rest. She tries to locate ancient cities in the storm, convinced that some Nepalese demon is causing the mirage of emptiness. A cruel game to force Jeanne and her to abort their life-giving rescue mission.

Standing still, Rachel feels the tension of the scarf. The scarf that yanks her out of the game. Then, she feels the slack. And her cousin emerges from the white.

Jeanne waves her arms in defeat: I lost it.

The game? Me too.

The trail. I don't know where to go.

They look around. In this white desert where earth, sky, trees merge into nothingness, they have lost their bearings. Below, the city has vanished. The overcast sky hangs so low, it obliterates the street lights from view and robs them of any means of orientation. Try as they may, they can't make out anything. Streets, lights, the squat blocks of red brick houses. All gone. They can't even hear traffic.

Rachel guesses that they have been walking in circles for an hour. An hour! Far from home! And lost! She glares at Jeanne. If she had brought her play shovel, she would use it this minute to whack some sense into her cousin's head.

Jeanne looks ahead. Points: The lodge. That way.

The lodge! Stupid! We can't even see the city. How can you know where the lodge is in this? This time, you really did it, Jeanne! Mom will be...

They'll be super late for supper. Rachel knows it. At home, her mom is fretting. Pearl checking her watch every five minutes. Peering out the window. Searching the snowy night. Phoning Rachel's and Jeanne's friends. At the moment, Rachel can't remember if, in the rush of departure, she even told her mom where they were going. To go play up Mount Royal without first asking permission? Jeanne would have replied that they wouldn't be gone long, they'd be back in plenty of time for supper, let's go. Chilled to the bone, Rachel will die here. And so will Jeanne! Good! That'll teach her. They'll die, both as alone and forgotten as their parents were. Rachel who forgot to be a good girl. Pearl fretting.

Rachel's face covered in snow, eyes brimming with wind-whipped tears, she searches for the dark shape of the lodge. Tonight in the alien surroundings, she experiences the same disorientation as she does in her dark bedroom in the middle of the night when she has to get up, half asleep, walking round and round, unable to find the door or the furniture until she manages to turn on the lamp. Here, she hasn't got the luxury of electricity within reach, and yet, she must get somewhere.

She shivers with cold and dread. Still holding the cord tied to the toboggan, the cord twisted around her mitt and numbing her fingers, she lets out a mad little laugh. Such trouble for nothing. All that snow, and they aren't even sliding. And yet, despite the lack of blood flow in her fingers, Rachel will not let go of her toy. The sled, a raft without which she will sink into the white sea.

Through the slits of her nearly closed eyes, she spots something. Points with her free hand: Over there, Jeanne. Over there, that's the lodge, yes?

Jeanne confirms her cousin's discovery with hoots. The girls run, spit out snowflakes and, out of breath, reach the dark mass of the stone lodge that appears out of the snow.

Jeanne unties the red scarf that has kept them together. Rachel disentangles the cord from her hand, her piece of wreckage that allowed her to arrive safe and sound. Against the stone wall, the wind relents and the cousins can breathe to their lungs' content. Sweat drips down their spines and their teeth are chattering.

We must get in, Rach.

How?

They go around the lodge. Shake door handles. Locked. Peer through windows. See only darkness. Call out. Nothing moves outside or inside.

Jeanne seizes the sled. But its long, narrow shape is too awkward for her to handle alone.

Help me.

Do what?

We'll ram it in this window like invaders in movies do with a log to break down the castle door.

Are you crazy?

Cold. I am cold. And I need a pee.

Me too.

Rach, I can't do this alone.

Rachel, who never gets into trouble, helps Jeanne, who often gets into trouble. They lift the back end of the sled. At the count of three they run, and ram the curled front into the low window. They have to try five times. On the fifth try, Rachel knows they're in a pile of shit.

Glass breaking. Clear sound above monotone wail of wind. Gaping hole surrounded by a thousand fissures. Next will appear security guard in black uniform. Grabbing the vandal cousins by the scruff of the neck. Jail, you two!

Damn you, Jeanne!

You're always afraid of getting punished or scolded or...

My toboggan! You broke my toboggan.

They stare at the twisted toboggan, half-hanging through the smashed window.

We had no choice, Rachel.

No choice? We could have found a better way.

And freeze while searching?

With you, it's always...

It's either die outside or save ourselves inside. Jeanne slides the useless sled into the snow.

You never think before...

Go in, and careful with the glass.

As soon as Rachel feels the warmth on her face, her qualms, fear, anger, they all melt as fast as the snow stuck to her clothing. She coos with relief. Her muscles, tense for so long, relax and she shivers, shivers.

The cousins take off mitts, scarves, tuques, coats. They cover the broken window with a large piece of cardboard advertising a giant strawberry ice cream cone.

Because of the snowstorm, the night outside has remained clear. Inside, the girls must walk with arms straight in front to guide them. Their fingers grope along walls to locate a switch.

I found one, Jeanne. Nothing.

It's dead here too. Must be a power failure.

Ouch, damn! Careful. I just hit my head.

Rachel touches the point of impact. Of course, she hit the injured spot.

It felt like, a, locker or something, Jeanne. Metal.

Jeanne laughs: I can't see you. Where are you hiding?

Wait. I'll go stand in front of a window.

Before a hand grabs her, Rachel hears the sound of a collision. A laugh and a curse. Now holding hands, their free arms straight out, the girls find the curving stairway that leads to the snack bar. At last, they reach the higher floor. Up here, the panoramic windows cut through darkness in big slices.

Rachel marvels: Look at that snow! A real blizzard like they had in the days of Nouvelle-France. You know. The colonists were trapped inside their houses for days.

Nose against the window, her face wrapped in the fog of her breath condensing on cold glass, Rachel can't get enough.

Jeanne, do you think we'll have to spend the entire night here?

Isn't it great! The whole place to ourselves. Jeanne moves things around behind the counter: And no one telling us what to do.

We had the mountain to ourselves. And look what happened. I nearly split open my head and you broke my toboggan. What are you doing?

Rachel walks toward the darker shape of the counter, tripping against a chair leg before reaching her destination.

Ah, I found some. Jeanne strikes a match and fixes a candle in a small pool of melted wax. Soon, a luminous line flickers along the edge of the counter, which she wipes with an imaginary cloth: What may I serve you, Miss?

No no no no no! I won't play the customer. No! Move over. You be the customer.

As Rachel enters the light, Jeanne shrieks.

Shriek all you want. I'm telling you, I won't be the customer, Jeanne. You're always d'Artagnan or the Warrior Queen. This time, I'll be the important character. I'll be the server.

That's not it. It's your face.

My face? Scrunching her muscles into a scary mask made scarier in the candlelight, she plays ghost, enunciating each syllable: This is a phan-tas-ma-go-ri-cal face for a phan-tas-ma-go-ri-cal night.

Jeanne shrieks for the fun of it, then sobers up: Your face. It's covered in blood. That's what's scary.

Rachel touches her forehead, crusted over. She finds a mirror hanging on a pillar. In the candlelight, her puffed-up face and her left eye, swollen half-shut, shock her to death. Now that she sees it, the deep cut throbs intensely.

It's your fault, Jeanne. Because of you, I'll have a huge scar. And what if I go blind in that eye? It's all your fault.

Let me wash off the blood and wrap a towel around.

Jeanne finds a white linen towel and a white apron. At the deep sink behind the counter, she wets the towel and cleans the wound. Despite the pain, Rachel tries not to squirm, practising making herself tough. Jeanne wraps the towel around her cousin's forehead. Folding the apron, she secures the bandage in place with the apron strings. At the same time, they both remember they need to pee.

On a dare, they enter the men's washroom, propping the door open to let in some light. The girls stare at the urinals, hooting at the contraptions. Rachel, who hates sitting down on public toilets, pees standing up. Jeanne follows her cousin's lead. Their aim not too good; they splash their boots. Share their rather limited knowledge of male anatomy. Still, while rinsing their boots in the bathroom sink, Rachel declares urinals a more hygienic way to pee in public toilets.

Yes, Rach, but. There's no privacy and you're shy about...

That's true. Rachel hadn't thought about that. Men though. Maybe they enjoy peeing together. Maybe they have contests. That's the disadvantage of growing up without fathers. You can't ask them important questions.

Back in the main room, Jeanne admires her handiwork in the candlelight: Rach, you look like a soldier wounded in real battle.

Rachel examines herself in the mirror. Even though her swollen eye worries her, the overall effect of the white bandage pleases her. She also has mixed feelings about this place. So ordinary when the server prepares the hot dog and hot chocolate that Rachel's mother orders her after she's come in from skating, and yet, so mysterious tonight, as to...

Gongs and chimes suddenly sounding in the silence make her jump. She turns around. Jeanne with her flair for the dramatic. Banging on gigantic stainless steel mixing bowls. Causing the oversized spatulas hanging over the grill to collide into one another. Next, she wouldn't be surprised to see her daffy cousin juggle with the chef's knives, shiny blades flashing in the candlelight. Or wear as a fencing mask one of the empty metal frying sieves hooked over their basins of congealed grease.

Jeanne hoots: Wait till we tell this story at school! Our big winter night in this place. The Christmas pageant will be a flop compared to our adventure. Everybody'll be so jealous. You can bet on it. I'm hungry.

Without missing a beat, she goes in search of food, her partner in adventure following closely.

They open the heavy wooden door of the fridge. The kind you walk in! Select milk—no, no, not milk, not on a night like this!—hamburger buns, minced beef already formed in patties. Rummage through shelves for pastries that taste of grease and artificial vanilla, so yummy. Get two Cokes out of the cooler.

Take notes, Rach, because we'll propose this night as the official school pageant. As soon as we get home, we'll begin writing the play.

As Rachel bites into her ketchup-loaded hamburger, her stomach tightens. But nothing in the world will keep her from eating this meal to the last morsel. Prepared on a restaurant gas stove. (And they're only eleven and they didn't burn themselves.) In a deserted public lodge. Where they had to break a window. (Oh, her poor toboggan!) So the cousins could find shelter. While a snowstorm. While a *huge* snowstorm was raging. The whole night. Alone together. Cut off from all adults. And left to their own re-source-ful-ness. She bites into her hamburger and must admit, Jeanne is queen of the game. Swallows. Takes another bite. If Jeanne hadn't been with her, Rachel would still be wandering. Lost and freezing in the storm. Swallows. Yes, but. If it hadn't been for Jeanne, Rachel would be having supper with her mom right now and none of this...

Rach, isn't this night the most marvellous night of our entire lives! Beating Christmas by a long shot.

Rachel isn't so sure. She bites into a May West. Before the night ends, her mom will die of worry. Licking the yellow cream from between the two layers of the little cake, she sees it all. Pearl making urgent calls. Getting no help. Weeping. Lamenting her daughter buried under snow as her husband was. The thought of her father ruins Rachel's dissecting even more than the thought of her mother's panic.

It's true, eh, Jeanne? Mothers are the queens of worry.

I wouldn't know that, now, would I?

Oops, sorry. Even if grown-ups don't think so, we can take care of ourselves.

You bet, we can.

As Jeanne tears the cellophane wrapper off a Twinkie, the ringing of a phone shatters the silence. Fills the space with roaring outrage. Caught in the act of stealing, breaking and entering, vandalism, the cousins jump off their chairs in a panic, screeching like back-alley tomcats in the night.

Jeanne shouts above the insistent tumult: Where's the damn phone?

Don't answer. It can't be for us. If we answer, they'll know we broke in. We didn't steal anything. But. We'll still go to jail.

Jeanne is as helpless to deal with the situation as Rachel, until she has a brilliant idea: What if it's your mom? She knows we came to Mount Royal to slide.

She does? I don't remember telling her.

Since we're not home yet and it's late and it's snowing like in the days of New France, she would phone the lodge, right?

Don't answer, Jeanne! It can't be Mom. Don't answer!

The phone goes on ringing, urgent, menacing, accusing. Jail! Jail! Jail!

We *must* answer.

No!

If we don't, it would be like refusing help while drowning.

We are not drowning.

I found it.

Jeanne, no!

Hello? At first, her voice, so unsure, produces no more than a high-pitch mew, until it brightens into relief: Auntie Pearl! I knew it was you. It's your mom, Rach. See? I was right. Yes, yes, Auntie. This is Jeanne speaking.

Rachel moves closer to the phone, putting her hand over the mouthpiece: Tell Mom everything's fine. Don't say anything about. And she touches her bandaged head.

Jeanne nods, indicates to Rachel to keep quiet for a moment, then speaks into the mouthpiece: We're both okay, Auntie Pearl. But we had to break a window to get in. It was a matter of life or death... You're sure they'll understand?... There's no electricity, but we found candles and we made hamburgers on the gas stove... Of course, we were careful. You taught us well... No, it's still warm in here. When will you be able to come and get us?... Oh, yes? All night?... She's here. Your mom wants to talk to you.

Hi, Mom! Rachel is somewhat disappointed to detect no hysteria in her mom's voice, only a minor worry put to rest: Yes, Mom, we'll be careful. Do you think they'll make us pay for the hamburgers?... We also ate some cakes. Little ones... What about the broken glass? It's a big window... And my toboggan. I'll tell you later... No, nothing... Don't worry, Mommy. We'll keep warm. See you tomorrow. Bye.

Rachel joins Jeanne at their table piled with ketchup-smeared paper napkins and cellophane wrappers.

Mom says a lot of the streets are closed because of the snow. There are power failures all over Montréal. Even on the south shore. They won't be able to fetch us until tomorrow.

The accomplices burst out laughing. Then they allow silence to measure for them the full scope of the event.

After a while, Jeanne speaks, her voice husky: We're lucky to have the lodge. Your dad and my mom didn't have such luck.

Rachel's voice is quiet: When we were lost in the snow and I was getting really cold, I was thinking about them. I was playing the game. We were searching for them and we rescued them.

I was playing the game too. I wonder if it's easier to freeze to death. Or to drown. Or to die in a boiling jungle.

Albert and Colette could have died a thousand different ways, like in stories.

This is not a story, Rachel.

No.

Jeanne creases the cellophane. She rolls it into a tight ball and, as soon as she lets go of it, it puffs up. She pursues, her voice hoarse: When my mom came back from her endless expeditions and we spent a few weeks together, she was always telling me stories about the jungle.

In the jungle, Jeanne, there are tigers. Colette and Albert could have been attacked and devoured by a big tiger. It must be scary being eaten by a tiger.

It would hurt like crazy. My mom and your dad also spent months in all sorts of deserts, remember. In Africa. In Australia. In Asia.

I know that.

In their deserts, they could have died of thirst, like in adventure movies. They say when you're that thirsty, your tongue swells up like a balloon.

It's worse dying of thirst if you're in the middle of the ocean. Like when your ship sinks and you're stuck in a lifeboat or hanging on to a piece of wreckage, like in war movies. That much water around you, and not being able to drink. What torture!

I'm thirsty just thinking about it. Jeanne gets two bottles of Coke from the cooler.

And what about sharks, Jeanne? There are always sharks.

Rachel drinks and the fizz makes her burp. The girls launch into a burping contest. They burp and laugh until the game loses its appeal.

Jeanne pushes the tip of her tongue into the neck of the bottle: My mom told me. It happened once.

Sharks? They were attacked by sharks?

Jeanne pulls her tongue out of the bottle: Not sharks. Their boat capsized in a storm. They were lucky. Everybody managed to swim to a small coral reef.

Coral! It must be sharp. Did they cut their feet?

Rachel?

Yes?

Would you. Would you prefer to know for sure your dad is dead or would you prefer not to know? I mean for real?

I don't know, Jeanne. When Mom explained he was *declared* dead, I cried, but I wasn't really sad. I cried because I had to, otherwise Mom would have thought I didn't love him. I cried, and the more I cried, the more I wanted to cry. I liked the tears. But I'm telling you, Jeanne. If Mom had died, I would have cried my eyes out for really really real. A really huge real sadness.

Why so sad for Auntie Pearl and not for Uncle Albert?

Because. Because I didn't really know my father. He was away so much with Auntie Colette. Your mom. *The brother and the sister of the big expeditions.* Granny used to say that. So, when he came home, I felt bizarre around him.

Bizarre?

I don't know. Like those salesmen who ring our doorbell. Imagine one of them moving in with us. And Mom was all excited, paying more attention to him than to me. It's not that I was jealous, it's just. She was different when he was around. I couldn't wait for him to leave, even if it made Mom sad. And a little sharp with me for a while.

So, you're glad he's dead?

Rachel doesn't answer. Some things are best left to live in silence. But now, she is dying to ask *that* taboo question, even though her mom made her promise never to talk about *it.* So, she takes a deep breath: Your father, Jeanne. You never knew him, right?

You know I'm a bastard. And my mom never spoke about him. Maybe *she* didn't know him.

But. To have babies, the woman must know the man, right?

Maybe it's not necessary to know each other to make babies. Like when we buy penny candies at the corner store. We don't really know Mrs. What's-her-name. That doesn't stop her from selling us licorice and jawbreakers.

The cousins ponder this tricky question. After a while, Rachel breaks the silence: Colette was also *declared* dead. Why don't you believe it?

Jeanne stares at the large windows. Listens to the wind. Sees her mom's fleeting face against the white night, a face that is becoming increasingly blurry since the last visit. So long ago. She answers her cousin, her voice barely above a murmur: It's like Christmas, Rach. I'm looking forward to it for two months and, as the day gets closer, I become more and more excited. The most exciting moment is Christmas Eve at seven in the evening when we're going to bed. It's hard to fall asleep, but eventually, I do. Then at midnight, Auntie Pearl comes to wake us up. And the house is full of lights. And the Christmas tree and the presents. But an hour later, it's over. After we've opened our presents, it's not the same anymore. Even with the music and the candies and the special food, I'm sad.

Sad. Why sad?

Because it's over. But of course it's not. Sure, we must wait one whole long year for the excitement to begin all over again. But it will. When I'll know for sure Mom is truly dead, it will be truly over. It'll be over for real. *Declared* dead is not dead for sure. Your mom explained, it's dead on paper only. One day, I swear I'll know for sure. One day.

I understand. But Rachel keeps her real thoughts quiet. Truly, she does not understand Jeanne's desire. Rachel is certain that Colette is as dead as her own father. Over there in those terrible Himalayas that keep their bodies in the frozen hell. She shivers.

You're cold?

A little.

Me too. It's not so warm anymore. Let's get our coats. They must be dry by now.

The candles have burned themselves out, leaving on the counter pools of hardened wax. Lying down on the floor and facing the big windows to forget the darkness behind them, Jeanne and Rachel are wrapped into their coats. Not sleeping, not talking.

The wound on Rachel's forehead is throbbing. She wishes she could sleep and wake up with the morning. Against the thick sheet of snow, she sees shapes moving, running, hiding. A man in a black coat. A wolf. A vulture flying into the glass, clinging to it, vanishing. Fear pushes her against the floor. Keeps her from swallowing. The fear of nothing and everything. Don't be a crybaby, Jeanne told her many hours ago. Get tough, to prepare for the day when Jeanne will make you go into those terrible mountains. Prepare yourself, because when Jeanne wants something...

Suddenly, Rachel hears a tiny noise behind her. She concentrates on the sound amplifying itself. A rustling of cellophane. Muffled steps. A creak and a crack. A pop. Silence. She listens and hears the sounds again. Rustling. Muffled. Creak crack pop. And again and again. Her heart beats so fast she could throw up ketchup and greasy cake. She wants to cough but holds on until her eyes are swimming with tears.

Through clenched teeth, Jeanne whispers: You hear that?

Yeah.

Do you think he came in through the broken window?

Probably. And Rachel recalls the strange shadows in the snow. A man in a black coat. But also, a wolf and a vulture. She knows there are no wolves and no vultures on Mount Royal. But the man in a black coat? She whispers: Jeanne? You think it's the security man? Earlier, I saw...

Don't make a sound. Maybe he just wants to make himself a cup of coffee. To stay awake.

He'll see us. We should have cleaned up our mess. Now, he will have proof. We'll be arrested.

There's no electricity, Rach. He'll see nothing.

Security men have flashlights.

Not this one.

Then, it's not the security man. Jeanne? What if? It's a thief? Or worse. And Rachel remembers the big knives hanging above the stove. Holding her breath, she calls out: What are you doing?

Crawling away from those windows.

Don't leave me.

The cousins crawl into thicker darkness in a far corner of the room.

I'll pee in my pants, Rach.

And I'll throw up. I can't breathe. Listen.

I hear nothing.

It was just the wind.

If you say so, Rach.

As they relax, a popping sound louder than the previous ones makes them jump out of their skin. Then several pop-pop-pops in a row.

Rachel speculates: Same sounds as our pipes at home when they're farting inside the walls.

The noise stops only to resume a few seconds later.

Jeanne mutters: Sure. Must be the lodge trying to take off in the storm. Tomorrow, we'll wake up in those mountains. So very far away.

Exhausted, the girls lie down on the hard floor. Wrapped in their coats and getting used to the unexplained noises, they soon fall into a deep sleep. Toward dawn and through the morning, the cousins, without waking, huddle closer and closer together, as the cold takes over the lodge.

At midday, Jeanne and Rachel are startled out of their cold-induced sleep by blinding sunshine and the racket of a snow blower making its way toward the lodge. And what an aftermath! Pearl, carrying blankets and flasks of hot chocolate, is escorted by a policeman and a policewoman. The policewoman checks Rachel's wound, declaring that a trip to the hospital is mandatory. After something like an inquiry into the state of the place, and no blame laid on the girls, but praise from the policeman for their surviving the night, the cousins return home in the mighty snow-eater. Pearl promises a new shiny toboggan and the heater in the cab turns the girls into melting marshmallows.

Thanks to their photos in the newspapers, to the bandage and sutures on Rachel's forehead, the cousins become instant heroines at school, even though the ordinary pageant is presented instead of Jeanne's version of the winter tale.

That their story isn't staged doesn't deter Rachel from indulging in a nightly dissection of her grand adventure with her crazy cousin who had promised she would end up loving the game. And, of course, Rachel does. For a while, in the schoolyard, at the corner store, at the skating rink, kids watch them from afar, with admiration and with envy.

A few days later, used to stars living among them, the kids turn their attention to more pressing matters. After all, Christmas is getting closer and closer, and nothing can outshine that glitter. Even for Jeanne and Rachel. Except, of course, the eternal snow shining bright and deadly in the highest mountains in the world.

Kinabalu / Realm of the Cold

AT MIDNIGHT, on cue, the bungalow generator shuts down, jolting my brain out of sleep, and, before the blades of the overhead fan halt, I'm sweating like a sow in a smelting furnace.

In search of a breeze, I carry my sodden sheet to one of the veranda chairs, fully cognizant that the outside has no more air current than the inside. The only movement comes from the river flowing like molasses a few metres off. Although *flowing* is too energetic a word; the brown water seems as static as if frozen. That's what I was dreaming. Ice along the shore, and me, immersed in glacial water. A dream of the Great White North of home. People do die of heat exhaustion. And I have been *living* (too perky a word) in a state of heat prostration for three dangerous days.

Three days ago, the young woman who cooks and cleans told me the doctor was away collecting. Collecting? How long does collecting take? The young woman was so sorry, but the doctor had not informed her that the doctor's gentleman friend was coming. Not informed her? Well, not *not* informed her, but there was great excitement, what with

Kadazan man who was extinct and wild goose chase in ravine and rebirth of old plant... The young woman would do her best to make my wait a pleasant one. And once or twice, when I attempted to make sense of what she was trying to tell me, gently coaxing her to give me more details, she went on rambling about an urgency, what with babi and open wound and rush back to village and and... So, I let her be.

Still, none of it explains... A forest sound like a rusty hinge on a rubbish bin lid derails my thoughts. A night bird? Something fierce with claws? In the jungle cacophony, this call is new to me. Your dearest friend calls to invite you to her Borneo paradise, then goes *collecting*? Leaving you by yourself to fend off this green inferno? Not like Sab, that, to forget, to ignore, to dismiss, to neglect. I crumple into my chair and my predicament.

Another animal's cry mimics water dripping into a puddle. This I've been hearing for three nights; quite mesmerizing. Then come more familiar sounds. Dogs barking and fighting, followed by drunken men slamming car doors, slurring and giggling. In their nightly pantomime, the men get into a dugout and paddle across the molasses river toward their village. Soon after, the generator on the opposite bank stops, switching off the few light bulbs. Darkness falls thick as coffee grounds. Around the compound, free-roaming roosters flap their wings and crow in ear-splitting canon, cueing the dogs to bark and snarl anew. I sweat misery. Cramps in the belly. Body temperature rising. The beginning of a headache. I must rehydrate. Fresh lime juice is an excellent quencher to offset the effect of my overactive sweat glands. I would get up to drink, but I'm too impaired to stand on my swollen feet.

The racket of a freight train. The first night, it jerked me upright in the chair. Later, I learned that there is no train, or as they say locally, no tren, in this region. The nightly barge propels its way downriver, its high beam bleaching the jungle, its motor roaring louder as it approaches, decreasing as the boat slides into the distance. Monkeys scream. More barking and more crowing. In darkness restored, I feel the feather touch of *Anopheles* on my arm, hear their high-pitched buzzing as they land on my face. I dive under the sheet. Can't breathe. Heart rate increasing. This heat attacks as physically as any claw or poisonous bite. I must go in search of a cure for the shock of heat, otherwise I'll croak before the cock crows. I mean at dawn as it's supposed to be. Despite Sab's absence puzzling and worrying me, I must deal with my situation. For now, shivering is the only pursuit. Cold, the only cure.

At first light, I wake up the village teksi driver, requesting that he drive me to Kota Kinabalu, paying the extra fee for the optional air conditioning. I throw my pack in the boot and sprawl out on the back seat. En route, I am carried, body and soul, in the cool chariot of felicity. Heat is akin to pain. No matter how excruciating it was, once gone, it becomes an abstraction. K.K., located on the northwest coast of Borneo on the South China Sea, is no abstraction. On the coast, my chances of catching a breeze, albeit a sizzling one, may increase; in any case, the city will guarantee more miserable heat. Fortunately, being the capital of the state of Sabah, K.K. will be appointed with air-conditioned hotels. From one of those havens, I'll phone the bungalow daily. Until the housekeeper announces that the doctor has returned from collecting. Until Sab grabs the phone from her and hoots in my ear to get my ass over there pronto. Leaning my head against the backrest, I relax. Salvation is close at hand.

Two men flag down the teksi, a mode of transportation people share in this part of the world. The men belong to the Orang Ulu tribe. Handing me the tuak, one of them tells me in good English that his longhouse is nearby, stopping short of inviting me over, although passing me the bottle.

Early morning sweet rice wine, in my state of dehydration after a string of sleepless, sweaty nights, could only bring on a debilitating headache. But drink I do, for refusing may offend. Good-natured, the men declare they don't sweat. As if to prove the point, after veering off the highway into a rutted lane, they leave the air-conditioned car when we reach a tin-roofed shack. The sun-bleached sign reads Titman Yee Hoe Chicks & Dry Goods. I would have elected to wait in the cool car, but the teksi driver joins in with his passengers, turning off the motor. I am enthusiastically invited to this tribal grocery shopping expedition. To refuse may offend. So, off I go into the dreaded heat.

We enter Titman Yee's shop the way pies enter the oven. Dough-white, I'll be baked to a golden hue upon exit. The trio nods at the shopkeeper slouched behind the counter piled high with dry goods. I have yet to see or hear chicks. The Orang Ulu men use the driver and me as shopping carts. Our arms become heavy with sos cili, babi loin and karbau ribs, soursops, mangosteens, green coconuts, many fragrant leafy vegetables our northern supermarkets never stock. Last but not least, a twelve-pack of pahit, the soft drink looking conspicuously like tonic water. Which it is, according to the Orang Ulu man with good English. He educates me.

You see, "pahit" means bitter in Malay. Tonic water used to contain a fair bit of quinine. To ward off malaria. That's what the colonials believed. Quinine is bitter-tasting, hence the word "pahit," as in their gin pahit, which they drank in large quantities.

And recalling the Somerset Maugham stories set in these parts, I ask if the quinine did ward off malaria.

The Orang Ulu man grins and the *Anopheles* of the last three nights come back to haunt me. And Sab out there, collecting her plants to study their professed medicinal properties, could she provide a better prophylactic than my prescription of chloroquine? And to help me understand the process, she would draw the chemical structure on a napkin or in the sand. A wave of hotter air hits me, making me dizzy. To keep me from harbouring pahit-ness toward Sabourin for her vanishing act (which I realize in my dizzy spell is annoying me more than I want to admit) and for putting me in the position of developing malaria on her veranda and in a futile attempt to forget that the confinement of Titman Yee's shop is baking me fiercely, I pursue my education of market Malay words. Learning that "babi" is pig and "karbau" water buffalo and that "ketjap manis," as in ketchup, is, logically, sweet soy sauce, and assuming that "sos cili" is chili sauce. Discovering that many Malay words very much play on the ear a game of corruption of the English language. A playfulness that pleases me. Pleasantry aside, I'm still sweating like a babi. And I sense a new source of irritation in the groin.

I glance at the display of poskads, but must avert my eyes, as each beautiful view of Borneo emphasizes linguistic torment, bringing to mind such words as sultry and scorching, steamy and scalding, blazing, broiling or plain hot that make me reel. Do the Malays have as many words for heat as our Inuit have for snow?

The second Orang Ulu man orders four plastic cups of vanilla ais krim. Ais krim! What must I do to convince Titman Yee to allow me to curl up in his freezer, how many ringgits would that request set me back? I'm not seeking a full night stay, a quickie ten-minute reprieve would do nicely. What must I do?

Oh, to feel again the froidure of the Columbia Icefield of my northern country. Right now, I watch the ice of my dessert lose its hardness in the heat, collapse under its garnish of sweet red bean paste and condensed milk the shopkeeper slathers in silence into the cups. I am suddenly aware that the silence in ovens and churches has the same quality. Churchgoers collapsing in a heap, not as the result of religious ecstasy, but from heatstroke.

Back on the road, and in the felicity of the cooling car, eating my sickly sweet treat, I note that the Orang Ulu men's clothes and skin are bone-dry, but that the teksi driver wipes his forehead with a kerchief. Aha, not a tribal man. And neither am I. When I manage to connect with Sab, I must ask her how a northern gal can bear it in this country. And this irritation in the groin is intensifying. For relief, I sit on the edge of the seat, legs wide apart, careful not to graze the knee of the Orang Ulu man with good English, sitting in the back seat with me.

Artificial coolness on my face and arms, I pretend that Sab is the one sitting beside me in this icebox on wheels. And together, we enjoy the poskad views of her paradise. Daredevil dogs, or since no vehicle slows down for them, suicidal canines ambling across the road. Safer on the shoulder, horses and goats feeding on grasses. Against weather-beaten houses, the impossibly white clothes of Malaysia drying on clotheslines. In a field, cows glistening with sweat, chewing their cud under the savage sun. Entering Kota Kinabalu. Bidding au revoir to my travel companions and settling the fare with the driver, I jump from cool Mazda to cool Mangosteen Inn.

Checking in. Clean and air-conditioned. Kinda seedy in the grand manner of the tropics. From my room, I phone the bungalow to let the housekeeper know where I am. Must make a trunk call.

Good afternoon, I wanted to know if Sab was back?

Sarawak?

What?

Yes, Sarawak State south of here.

No, no, I mean the doctor. Is Doctor Sabourin back yet?

Doctor still away collecting.

Yes, but the doctor knew her friend from Canada was coming, yes?

But there was urgent...

Ah... The rebirth of the old plant?

Yes, very rare. Doctor had to go.

Now that the young woman seems calmer, I'm starting to understand why Sab stood me up. And I can piece together the puzzle of the last three days, minus the housekeeper waving her arms toward the deep jungle and uttering a confusion of Malay words. So, I surmise a Kadazan man came to the bungalow to report to Sab that a rare plant, believed to be extinct, was spotted growing in a ravine in the jungle. Sab had to go check this out, mindful that it might be a wild goose chase. But there may be more to this reasonable sequence of events, and I must know. One of the words the young woman kept repeating was "babi" and now that I know what it means, I'm wondering.

On the phone, I articulate clearly: Are there wild babi in the jungle?

Yes, babi, very dangerous. The housekeeper is sputtering again, she had to rush back to her village to tend to...

I cut her off to shout in the mouthpiece: Sab has been injured by a babi? Had to be carried from the bungalow to where? A village hospital?

And slowly, the housekeeper thanks me for my concerns, but her brother will be all right.

The housekeeper's brother was the one who was gored by a babi?

Yes, brother will be fine, very bad in belly, but will be fine.

The clearer situation still leaves me with one question: I understand. Thank you. But tell me. Why did the doctor not leave a written message for me, her friend who has come all the way from Canada, at the doctor's invitation?

This bit of simple reasoning is met with dead silence, then heavy breathing, then a plea not to ask any more questions, it is not the housekeeper's place to interfere in the private affairs of the doctor, please.

Okay, I'm not here to give the poor woman the third degree; and certainly not in this heat. I apologize and she thanks me, insisting that the doctor will be back soon.

I wish her a nice day and put down the receiver. Have a nice day in your steam bath.

I need a cold shower. Strip and freak right out. My hairy chest and belly are covered in prickly heat. Even my penis. Now, that worries me. Sab might recommend an ointment extracted from some jungle roots or the application of curative leaves. To me, the best cure remains the cold compress of Canada. Nothing short of sinking into an alpine tarn would stop my sweat glands from overheating. A long cold shower could do the trick. Unfortunately, the single tap delivers only lukewarm water. I linger under that shower.

Naked as a badly skinned rabbit, with fur still on the chest and its flesh covered in raised red itchy spots, I pull back the sheet. Gingerly lie down flat on my back. Spread-eagled. Motionless. Fall into a deep sleep. Dreamless.

Wake up with a splitting headache. Examine my dick. Seems okay. But notice an angry blister or pimple the size of a marble in the right-side groin. The seat of the earlier irritation. Squeeze it. Swollen and painful. It oozes a little. Can't make head or tail of it. One of those horrendous tropical parasites that pierces its way through your skin and reproduces inside of you? I dab the growth with rubbing alcohol from my first-aid kit and stick a Band-Aid over it. Should phone the bungalow. If Sab is back, no doubt she will have an explanation and a suggested treatment. But it's siesta time in the jungle and I wouldn't want to disturb the already distraught housekeeper.

Instead, I duck into the heat of the afternoon. In three minutes, my T-shirt is soaked. Walk along the waterfront. South China Sea. The romance of the tropics. Fish being off-loaded and processed. Offal and other garbage thrown into the sea. Amines, Sab once told me, are a class of compounds found in rotting fish, which accounts for that characteristic smell. Amines prosper here.

▲ Kids swim in a lagoon. I would join the sea urchins if the water appeared less polluted. But I drag my soaked ass back to the hotel. Guzzle a beer in the bar. Go back to my cooler. Wrap a towel around my head, slip under the sheet and have a snooze to catch up from the previous sleepless nights.

In the evening, I eat laksa, fried squid and curried prawn. Nurse four beers. Watch the locals at their lives. Friendly, helpful, always smiling, nobody hassles you, nobody seems to quarrel. Malays, Chinese, tribespeople. A large Muslim population; the men wearing black felt caps and the women colourful hijab-like scarves.

Still hot and humid. The unbearable country of the single season. You're dripping wet within minutes of walking. Men in impeccably laundered white clothes are resting beside dilapidated houses. At the night market, I buy a pineapple and a durian. The pineapple, because it's so perfectly ripe, the scent as never I have smelled it, I had to have it. The durian, because of its reputation. A scary-looking fruit, durian, the size of a honeydew melon. This one specimen weighs five pounds on the scale.

Native to Malaysia, the vendor proudly reveals. A dozen species available. Tonight, only this one kind. He further impresses me with the fact that it is the only fruit tigerly enough for tigers to crave. And he stresses that I must hide Tiger's favourite in my small pack. Not allowed in hotels, airports or airplanes. Because of the fruit's foul odour once opened. Or because, I tell him,

wielded as a weapon, the hard spiky shell could cause serious
bodily harm. In turn, he quips that anyone unfortunate enough
to fall asleep under a durian tree wakes up with a sorry tale to
tell. With a twinkle in his eye, the vendor hands me the original
forbidden fruit.

At the speed of a West Coast slug, swollen groin making
walking uncomfortable, I ambulate back to the hotel taking in
the pleasant side of the city. Broken sidewalks and open sewers.
From everything rise effluvia of vegetation rot, rendered so
very sharp in the infernal heat. Sab walking by my side. Cool,
uncomplicated. Cerebral Sab not hampered by emotional
baggage. She may speak brusquely, but she also knows how
to listen. And always ready to share knowledge. To many, her
exact logical mind pegs her as a cold fish. Those people fail to
appreciate how low-maintenance she is. And that, above all, is so
refreshing. And at the moment, I could use a large dose of Sab's
coolness. In this suffocating country, where could she be?

In the hotel lobby, several whorish-looking girls are loitering.
Ah, the Sultry Woman of the tropics. This hotel either moonlights
as a brothel in the evening or a wedding reception is in progress
in the ballroom.

▲ Up at seven A.M. to take advantage of cool morning. Cool? Not
a chance! Two steps from the equator, the country has but one
season of sameness.

I should phone the bungalow again. Sab may be back from
collecting, slouched in one of the big chairs on her veranda,
pahit in hand, watching the molasses river *flow* by, wondering
where I might be. At least I have good news. The red welts are
more subdued after the night in my air-conditioned room. And
my dick is pale again. Though unfortunately, the growth on my
groin is not abating.

Eat dim sun in a small Chinese shop around the corner from the hotel. The only coolness provided by the ceiling fan. More like churning river water to fool you into believing it's drinkable. On the wall, posters warn about a cholera epidemic.

Stroll to a square lined with minibuses. Several teenage boys converge toward me. They call themselves runners. Their job is to hustle potential passengers.

Bas, mister? Bas, mister?

It would be erroneous to call them barkers since they practise their trade without shouting.

Bas?

They point at the minibuses.

And where do these bases go, might I ask?

Everywhere. Where you want to go, mister?

Anywhere cool?

Cool?

I'm seriously considering flying right back home to go lie down on the Columbia Icefield. Contrary spirits. At the equator, dreaming of snow; back home in February, pining for palm trees. The boys yank me out of my wintry rêverie by suggesting a few cool places. A temple complex on the outskirts of town. The botanical garden and the herbarium with many species of medicinal plants. A newly opened high-tech disco. Declaring the third point of interest the coolest.

Since plants with medicinal properties are right up Sabourin's alley, the staff at the herbarium may know the doctor's whereabouts. Beware! A tropical botanical garden promises more steamy heat. Will break out in hives again.

The eldest runner affirms with a smile: All cool places, mister.

The others acquiesce: All cool.

No no. Cool as in. And I mime shivering.

They immediately point up and away: Kinabalu, mister.

Kinabalu here. I point at my feet and mime dying of heat.

They laugh: No no, mister. Here is K.K. There is Gunung Kinabalu.

The eldest recites the lesson: "Kota" means town in Malay. Here is Kota Kinabalu. Over there is Mount Kinabalu.

Nabalu, spirits of the dead. That contribution from the shyest runner.

And it's cool?

They all assent energetically.

Again, the eldest runner provides vital information: Top of mountain is over four thousand metres above sea.

This is encouraging. If the boy's pitch is to be believed. Even so near the equator, at that altitude, I may catch a few hours of shivering. Hypothermia in Borneo; what a novel idea! And not a bad place to wait for Sabourin to return from her rare plant collecting expedition, or wild goose chase.

Is it far?

Seventy kilometres from coast. Two hours by bas. Good sealed road. Eight ringgits one way. Cheap.

Okay, pal, you made a sale. Which bas goes to Gunung Kinabalu?

He leads me by the elbow to one of the minibuses, while the other runners fan out, resuming their work hustling potential passengers.

I can't go right away. First, I have to get my stuff at the hotel and check out. When will the next bas leave?

We wait.

How long?

Until you finish at hotel. No rush.

But, not believing they will wait too long, I do rush. Half an hour later, drenched and laden with my possessions stowed into my large backpack, including the pineapple and the well-camouflaged durian, I hop on the bas, which duly departs, now that the twelve seats have been filled.

I enjoy more poskad views. The suburbs of the state capital feature a mixture of decrepit houses on stilts surrounded by fields full of scrapped cars and assorted junk, chickens and roosters running loose among the refuse. Reminds me of the Québec countryside of my childhood, minus the free fowls and the extreme heat. Here and there rises a modern bungalow, complete with a new car amid the squalor. Mangy half-starved dogs with sores run rampant. Stunned water buffalo lie half-buried in black mud.

On the phone before I checked out, the housekeeper seemed a little baffled. Did she understand where I was going? Note? No, doctor left no note. No note. She was becoming agitated again. No no, *I* want to leave a note *for* the doctor. Can you write this down? She claimed she had no pen nearby. Silly me! What if she can't read or write? Not true. I saw her read a magazine. No doubt, it was in Malay. I thought of suggesting that she write the note in Malay, but simply wished her a good day and hoped for the best.

Soon, the road climbs toward the mountain. Rising abruptly, its massive form dominates our field of vision even though clouds cap its summit. As the air cools, the anticipation is positively erotic. This mountain better deliver. For about twenty kilometres, we ascend almost continuously. As the boy promised, the highway is a relatively good road, but with hairpin turns and steep grades made the more entertaining each time the driver passes on blind curves. In fact, the runner withheld the small detail that the driver passes only on blind curves. Each time he performs that stunt, I concentrate on the mountain. Spirits of the dead, may you keep a kind eye on us.

I rent a large unadorned cabin with twin beds, a toilet dug into the floor and a shower that consists of a black garden hose

connected to a cistern full, I assume, of rainwater, and with a
veranda overlooking the jungle and surrounding hills. Except for
the vegetation and extreme humidity, this area of the national
park reminds me of Banff in the 1970s before it became crowded
and before hordes of Japanese and Chinese package tours
caused the price of lodging to skyrocket. My cabin costs forty-
two ringgits a night, about twenty bucks, and the place is not
crowded. Most visitors are Malaysians and other Asians from
neighbouring countries, along with a sprinkling of Europeans
and Americans. I'm told the park is gaining in popularity and
future expansion is planned. Banff in the seventies.

Twin beds. The daily afternoon rain begins. Would be so
fine if Sab showed up this instant. I fantasize that her plant
collecting had brought her to this side of the mountain. And
here she'd be. And we'd share this shelter as we did so many digs
in our university days. Barefoot on the veranda, cool gin pahit in
hand, passing a joint, surely, she could dig up some happiness-
enhancing plant out of her Borneo cornucopia that would do
the trick. And that wouldn't be trafficking in illicit substances,
exactly, an activity frowned upon in Malaysia. Those caught face
the death penalty. A stern message prominently displayed at all
ports of entry. Duly warned. Now, I am wondering if Sab didn't
duly warn the housekeeper not to worry me. Was it Sab who was
gored by the babi? Or searching for the impossible plant, did she
fall into the ravine and break all of her bones?

A little of Sab's simple logic helps me not to sweat it. If
nothing has happened, you've worried needlessly, all the while
putting your body chemistry out of whack. If something has
happened, no matter how high your level of anxiety, it has no
power to undo the event. There you have it. And so, I'm cooling
my heels at higher altitude until Sab's return. At least here, I'm
breathing for the first time in days. Then what? I bas back down
to that insufferable jungle? Would be so much better if she came

up to my version of the Borneo paradise. As tropical rain falls in the shadow of the mountain, we would yak up a storm about the wild old days, about her wild current days.

At The Canteen, from an eclectic and reasonably priced menu, I select a snack of chicken satay with a cucumber salad. Judging from the snippets of conversation I can understand, most visitors are here to climb the mountain. At the next table, five amiable Brits engage me in the usual conversation. As soon as I open my mouth, they peg me as German. Switch their demeanour to offhand.

German? Hell no. Why German?

Your accent.

It's French. I'm from Québec. Now a resident of Calgary. Western Canada.

They look as if they have committed a diplomatic blunder.

Don't worry, it happens a lot. I can't figure out why. Say, is it really cold at the top?

They laugh, friendly again: There's a true Canadian. Chasing blizzards in the tropics, eh?

At another table, a lone pasty-white man in his sixties. Australian, judging from his accent. What do I know? He may very well be an Icelander forever mistaken for an Aussie. Brandishing an arsenal of anecdotes involving chopsticks, he is showing his prowess to youngsters from Singapore. Mistaking my stare for an invitation, he makes a beeline for me just as I get up to leave. To avoid embarrassment, he strides in a wide semi-circle, pretending to aim for the other direction, and shouts a bright see-you-later-mates to the young Chinese men who, wasting no time, resume slurping their noodles, their chopsticks flying at lightning speed.

To educate myself, I take in a slide show on the history, geology, flora and fauna of Mount Kinabalu and the surrounding region, hosted by Dr. Chu, the head naturalist. That way, when

Sabourin and I manage to connect before my time on the island expires, I won't sound a complete nincompoop. Sab was the studious one, the brilliant one who investigated every source and every lead. No detail was too picayune to neglect. Moi, on the other hand, learned vicariously through her bottomless curiosity and her ability to process information quickly and correctly. Sab, the science A student with a major in chemistry, while I muddled through general studies, skipping classes in favour of playing my guitar and practising other people's songs. When she left Montréal to pursue post-graduate studies across the Atlantic in natural products chemistry, I was pretty miserable. I don't think I ever told her. On account of pride. The male's necessary aloofness. Nevertheless, her dedication to investigate plants at the molecular level impressed me so very much. Which didn't stop little moi from turning into a dilettante macroscoping his way through a collection of undistinguished occupations to earn a living. Did I disappoint her?

Dr. Chu raising her voice in annoyance yanks me out of my distraction. I missed several slides. She gets outraged, clicking through a series of shots illustrating the blatant exploitation of the resources of Borneo, particularly the destruction of the jungle, one of the oldest habitats of the world, home for millennia to a diverse people and to countless plants and animals. Dr. Chu's attitude is Sab's in the flesh. How many discussions of that nature have we had? Pursued through our uninterrupted correspondence over the years. I long for us to pick up the thread.

To the audience's astonishment, Dr. Chu shows spectacular slides of various species of *Nepenthes*, the famous carnivorous pitcher plants. A man in the front row pipes in about a *Nepenthes rajah* found in the nineteenth century by an English botanist who reported that it was thirty centimetres in diameter and contained two and a half litres of water and a drowned rat. The audience laughs and I recognize Mr. Australia showing off. Dr. Chu ties up her broken thread to present several slides of another star of the Malaysian jungle, the *Rafflesia*. A parasitic plant with no roots of its own that produces the largest flower on the planet. The Australian feels obliged to point out that when past its prime the flower smells like rotting flesh.

Dr. Chu instructs us that the smell of decay plays a direct role in the plant's reproduction, as it attracts flies and carrion beetles that carry the pollen from male to female flowers. My durian comes to mind. Should have asked the vendor how close to maturity it was before purchasing it. Dr. Chu pinches her lips before pointing out the paradox that Borneo has a large jungle forest industry, and yet, must import chopsticks. Pasty-white know-it-all is on a roll, now engaging the naturalist in his favourite topic. She indulges him, until the exchange turns to babble, then without pity, in Sab's style, she cuts him off to conclude the slide show. He rushes out of the room, announcing sudden urgent business.

Without pause, possibly to prevent the rest of the audience from streaming out, Dr. Chu begins a video about Mount Kinabalu itself, pointing out the unique flora that have captivated botanists since the nineteenth century. Today, scientists continue to gather plants on the slopes of the mountain and to discover new natural products. A challenging climb, judging from the rock formations. As long as I shiver, my goal will have been attained. Although, in walking steadily uphill, and, according to the video, on Gunung Kinabalu the uphill goes on a long way, you work up a sweat. I'm willing to take my pahit medicine to touch the cold.

And here she is! Sab's face appearing through the foliage. Sab holding a plant by the stem as by the neck, its root system dangling in mid-air. Sab, tall and grinning among her fellow plant hunters. And, unless this is a trick of light, not even sweating. As the video ends and Sab vanishes before my eyes, I jump to my feet.

When was this shot? I must know. Last year? This morning? I must know.

Half of the audience laughs; the other half gathers its belongings, ready to flee the madman. Dr. Chu reaches for a paging device to call security, the army, the death squad. They'll cart me away to the jungle loony bin where I'll sweat, forever sweat, in the realm of relentless humidity. Better beat a discreet retreat. Go lounge about at the cabin. Get into the proper tropical mode of zero exertion. Or should I go ahead and climb Gunung K.? And run into Sab? During my fantasizing earlier, my instincts must have told me she was nearby. In the video, tall Sab is still wearing her hair too short. It accentuates her awkward features.

Outside, as I'm weighing my options, the Australian catches up with me.

G'day, mate. You here to climb?

Haven't decided yet. You?

We gave this hill a burl more than once, the missus and me. Made it to the top too. Went everywhere with the missus. Those were the days. Nowadays, the old legs are a bit rooted. I better take it easy on shorter hikes. I can show you...

I may never return here. Might as well go for the top. Sorry.

No worries, mate. I'll give you a blow-by-blow description of what to expect. Care to join me for a pint or two?

Better turn in early.

And I leave him standing in the rain. What a cad I am. The man drips with loneliness. He mentioned a missus. His dear departed? Could be a case of divorce. Either way, poor sod. What would be the harm in keeping him company for an hour?

In the best tradition of mateship, two lone males in the jungle, swapping lies. As I'm reconsidering, it stops raining, and, he's gone.

Late afternoon, daylight dimming and a thick fog obscures hills and mountains. With nightfall begins the jungle symphony of birds and insects and mammals. I take a long shower. Go sit on the veranda. Watch the mist disperse.

Gazing at the equatorial sky, I recall something Sab once wrote to me about the physical world and why she thrives on the difficult questions that it poses. No one can put a spin on physical laws. They won't bend for anyone's convenience or agenda. With that in mind, I eat the intoxicatingly scented pineapple, letting the sweet-tart, sticky juice run down my chin and along my arm, feeding on one of nature's marvels. And how I marvel, this night, at the games we used to play without ever becoming a couple. And here I am, this night, perspiring with complicated pleasure. We were wise without knowing it. The sagacity of our youth preserved an enduring friendship.

Truthfully, I could not begin to imagine Sab as the missus. How about celebrating our wisdom with the durian? Is splitting the fruit open a forbidden act in a national park? Is this act also subject to the death penalty? I struggle to cut the shell open with my inadequate penknife. One needs a machete or tiger's fangs to get at the flesh. At the market, the vendor instructed me to discard the fleshy interior. You eat the heavy fibrous coating enveloping the several large seeds. I only managed to puncture the shell. If I keep at it, I risk impaling my wrist on the stiff stubby spikes that cover the devilish fruit. Better concentrate on the constellations.

▲ I slept, aware of tossing and turning. Skeins of dreams remain about Sab and giant flowers, and the stink of sewers in my nose.

This morning, I sniff the durian. So far, it is keeping its fetid self within its stubborn skin. All the same, to prevent olfactory catastrophe, I cover the knife cut with a Band-Aid. Not to be overlooked, the leftover pineapple scents the room shamelessly and the ants have found the bounty. I toss the fruit and its parasites into the trash can.

My joints feel stiff, as in a prelude to the flu. Merde! Not malaria. Those biting *Anopheles* on Sab's veranda. Merci beaucoup, chère amie! She lured me to the sick country, only to elude me. What madness, what sick game? Not like Sab, that! Overdosing on chloroquine won't repair damage already done.

Okay. I'm taking a deep breath. Must see the logic of the situation instead of imagining the worst without reason. I am waffling. Should I rest or would hiking to high altitude help to shake off whatever bug is exploring my system? It is still muggy, but the temperature is so much more bearable than at sea level. If I stay down, the Australian will want to buddy up with me. If I go hiking, I may run into Sab somewhere on the flank of the mountain. I put a small pack together. Since I'm checking out of my cabin, I'll leave my larger backpack in storage. And off I go to headquarters to register for the climb.

A bit of a free-for-all without the arguments. Hikers are massed by the counter with only one employee processing them. A little to the side a cluster of men stands quietly. The guides, I'm told. When my turn comes, I pay the fees for the climbing permit and for the compulsory services of a guide. Both are cheap, so no point arguing, even though I would prefer to walk the path by myself. And I spot the Australian.

You don't have to hire a guide, mate. They're not employees of the Park. They're freelancers. The missus and I sneaked in unnoticed. Many people do.

And if you're caught? Wouldn't that warrant the death penalty?

He guffaws at my quip: Too right! A few people get lost in the fog. Others pinch pitcher plants. Now, the missus, bless her soul, had a saying about...

See? The guides act as stewards of their domain. You can't blame them, considering they have to contend with humanity's stupidity and thieving tendencies. Besides, I already paid the fees.

This morning, he seems to be limping. I wish him a pleasant day, then acquaint myself with my personal guide.

Barely five feet tall, the man is all muscle and sinew gained and maintained, I gather, from continuous treks up and down the mountain. He is wearing light pants, a crisp short-sleeved cotton shirt and sturdy sandals. No socks. He's forty-two years of age, he tells me, as if that were a badge of honour or his certification as a competent guide. Unless it is an amazing age for a guide in these parts, and it might be. Revealing that I am also forty-two amuses him and I'm suddenly aware of my mini pot-belly, to say nothing of my many complaints since I landed in his country. I take this opportunity to inform him that I am French. To avoid having to explain later that I am not German.

Paris? And he mimes playing an accordion.

No no. Canada. That geographical shift confuses him: And you?

Dusun tribe.

And what does that mean?

Mean?

I have learned that "kota" means city and "kinabalu" means spirits of the dead.

In Malay. In Dusun language, aki nabalu. Aki is ancestor or grandfather. Nabalu is revered place of dead.

I stand corrected. And so. What does Dusun mean?

Dusun means Dusun. My name is Ebin. Just Ebin.

Pleased to meet you, Ebin. I'm Gilles Lanctôt. No meaning that I know of.

Jillanto. Hello.

When he reaches for my small pack, I notice he is carrying no gear at all.

Non non, thank you, non. Where I come from, we carry our own stuff.

He finds this custom curious, but, from my point of view if he carried my small load, I'd be the fat white man exploiting the Natives to do all the heavy lifting.

At eight A.M., a van transports us and several other hikers and their guides four kilometres to a power station where the road ends and the trailhead begins at 1,829 metres. As we set out, Ebin is suddenly laden with a metre-long cylinder which he carries over one shoulder, with no more effort than if it were a pillow. The ultimate water bottle. I'll need it too. We haven't gone five steps and already I'm dotting the trail with my salt water.

I point at the cylinder: That's a big water bottle. How many litres does it hold?

Water? No no, Jillanto. No. Propane gas. For cooking at rest house.

Silly me! Who has ever heard of compressed water? The guide educates me.

Food and cooking fuel carried up by hand. Garbage and empty cylinders carried back down by hand.

I bow to the man.

We start walking along a well-maintained forest trail, with wood planks driven crosswise into the ground, providing steps as well as slowing down the erosion caused by the daily rains. The terrain is steep from the start. No time to acclimatize calf muscles and lungs. I estimate the temperature at around 25°C, but with the humidex off the scale, I inform my guide about my condition.

Don't worry, Ebin. This is normal for me. I sweat buckets.

Also, and that I keep to myself, the swelling in the groin makes hiking painful.

Moss dangles from every surface and, on both sides of the trail, the trees grow dense. I expect madness lives in this kind of bushwhacking. Sabourin can bushwhack for days looking for her precious plants, and comes out unaffected by the experience. Once, I accompanied her on a gathering expedition in the interior of British Columbia. I maintained decorum, but, as I admitted afterward, the tick of looniness rode on the back of my neck the entire time.

At various elevations, we pass open shelters with tin roofs, each housing a tank that catches rain for drinking water. Ebin suggests I strap one of them to my back for my rehydrating needs. I appreciate his gentle deprecating humour. Thanks to last night's slide show, I recognize rhododendron shrubs, wondering if the plant has any medicinal properties. I notice that no one is collecting at the moment, covertly or officially.

Ebin points out a *Nepenthes villosa*: Jillanto, several species of carnivorous pitcher plant grow only on flanks of Aki Nabalu.

I acknowledge and huff and puff. Examine the pitcher plant up close, but see only Sab in that video holding the plant by the stem. Wishful thinking on my part, or is she truly collecting on this flank of Aki Nabalu?

Soon, the jungle makes way to temperate forest as we reach a telecom installation.

The guide informs me that we are at 2,225 metres and this is the Kamburongoh transmitter for Sabah telecom. He anticipates my question: Yes, Jillanto. Kamburongoh is Dusun word. And yes, it has meaning. Plant that wards off evil spirits.

Cooee, mate. It's been yonks since I jogged. The missus used to beat me easy. Ran marathons in her youth. Let herself go to seed in the end. Some three hundred metres higher, there's the Layang-Layang Sabah Radio and TV Station transmitter. And Layang-Layang, mate, means place of swallows. Don't mean to boast, but living in these parts on and off, one learns a thing or two.

I'm stunned that he managed to catch up to us. An old man on wobbly legs. He's red as a beet, but his skin appears dry as a cactus. I don't get it.

This seems as good a time and place to introduce myself. I'm Hugh Low.

Hulot? Monsieur Hulot?

That's right, mate. Hugh Low.

For the first time, Ebin shows lack of composure. Points at the mountaintop, points at the Aussie: Like Sir Hugh Low?

Too right! My namesake.

Namesake?

Yes, Jillanto. Sir Hugh Low made first recorded ascent of Gunung Aki Nabalu. 1851.

Interesting coincidence, wouldn't you say? One reason why I climbed the mountain so many times. The missus had it with it, but it feels like this mountain belongs to me. No bull dust. But like you, I'll probably never come back here. I'm getting on. And now, the missus gone. Well, you know how it is.

Ebin notices that mate man is without a guide, and I sure as hell don't wish to share mine, the spirit of mateship be damned. And so, I explain that, since we're not in the same party, the basic hiking protocol applies. To each his own pace. Besides, he shouldn't be on the mountain without a guide.

And he rails against Authority: The same, the world over.

While discreetly stretching the fabric of my shorts away from my groin, I agree: But, as well you know, when in Borneo...

No worries, mate. I shouldn't put you on the spot. Looks like you have a bit of trouble with the old sweat glands. And he points at his own crotch: Swollen sweat glands in the groin? The missus had that problem for years. On and off. Ninety days of antibiotics, nothing else would do. Wouldn't take medications. Finally relented. Cured her too.

Thanks for the advice. If I run into a druggist along the way, I'll stock up.

In these parts, mate, you can get them over the counter.

On that pharmaceutical note, I nod to my guide that we resume our uphill walk: Ebin, you people sure put your transmitters high up. You must have fantastic reception.

Reception, Jillanto? Yes. Our people like party, he quips.

I laugh and we push on, up and up without stopping, past the place of swallows. Soaked to the bone, I swallow from my water bottle, pleased that we have left the other hikers behind, relieved that monsieur Hulot isn't crowding us. (*Les vacances de M. Hulot.* I must see that film again one of these days. Are my own tropical vacances turning as ghastly as monsieur Hulot's seaside sojourn?) But where on this mountain will I find a cure for this heat attack? Better be soon. I'm running out of steam. Calf muscles cramping, just about every other muscle in spasm. Feeling a slight nausea too.

And I imagine Sab injured at the bottom of a ravine, days away from proper medical attention, the botanical wild goose chase ending in tragedy. The difference between us is that, while I see the monstrous whole as unmanageable, Sab has always had the ability to deal with each detail of the situation, no matter how complex. Not freaking out, as I would, at the prospect of a delicate extraction of the active compounds from a pile of plants. And, after she has finished to fractionate, as the technique is called, ending with one milligram of material in her vessel. The painstaking work. The coolness of procedure. And Jillanto on this mountain, with the summit still out of reach, should take heed. No wonder Sab became a natural products chemist, seeing the world at the molecular level. Maybe, that is intrinsic tranquility of mind.

▲ And just as my spirits are sinking, to say nothing of my weakening muscles, at about 3,000 metres, we gain a windswept ridge. The vegetation is stunted, of the scrubby alpine genus, and the view of the jungle valleys far below is truly dizzying, but here, I give myself entirely to the wind. Arms raised, I stand still, the wind drying clothes and skin, and I breathe. I breathe to the full in this revered place of the dead.

About an hour later, we reach treeline at Panar Laban. Perched at 3,353 metres on the southeast ridge of the mountain, the Laban Rata rest house is where we will stay until the middle of the night when we will complete the 748 metres to the summit.

Lunchtime, Jillanto. First people to climb to here, they sacrificed white rooster and eggs.

Sacrificed? Is that the Dusun word for lunch?

Jillanto makes joke. Very funny. Sacrifice means sacrifice. To appease spirits of mountain. Every year, some people repeat ritual.

What is to fear on this mountain, Ebin?

Mostly, Jillanto, superstitions. Also, getting lost in fog. Slipping and breaking bone. Falling off cliff. Getting hypothermia.

Hypothermia? Genuine full-blown hypothermia?

On summit. Very rare.

This is great, Ebin. Then, it does get that cold?

Ice on Aki Nabalu melted only ten thousand years ago. Cold still here.

That's good news, Ebin. But we sure didn't linger getting to this point. By my watch, it's now twelve thirty. Lunchtime indeed. Four and a half hours to cover only six kilometres, but with an elevation gain of over 1,500 metres and not forgetting evil humidity. My calf muscles tell me it's a lot. I'm pooped, but pleased.

My guide doesn't appear to be affected. He tells me his best time is four hours.

Great! I slowed you down only thirty minutes. Not bad, eh, Ebin?

He grins: No no, Jillanto. No. Four hours to summit and back.

You're kidding me.

Not so great.

Not that great! And how often do you go up and down Aki Nabalu?

Two, three times a week. Record is two hours and thirty-nine minutes.

Do you people jog up and down the mountain?

We have annual competition. Gurkhas from Nepal do well. Women compete too. Best time, six hours.

As I'm gazing at the two-storey rest house built in the shadow of towering cliffs near a stream cascading over a sheer rock face, I wonder what is Sab's personal best. In the play of light and shadow, I make out a face on the rock. Awkward features cut square in stone, a strong aquiline nose. My guide bids me a good stay until we undertake the night climb. And disappears from view, presumably, to deliver the cylinder of propane gas to the kitchen. Unless he has designs on some bird and eggs. Which I doubt, as he seems at peace with the mountain spirits.

Thick clouds gather, the wind blows and it begins to rain. The spirits spitting on me? The sudden cold startles me and I run to seek shelter. Stop, fool! And so, at 3,353 metres in the equatorial island of Borneo, the wind and rain of our northern Rockies have rushed in to greet me. I stand in the downpour. Shiver with delight. Let rain lave days of jungle sweat. Let rain cool down my feverish brain. I lie down on the wet rock. Offer myself to the spirits. A white Québécois cock sacrificing himself to secure the good will of the spirits of the mountain. Seven hundred and forty-eight metres below the summit, in their infinite kindness, the akis of Nabalu are granting Jillanto his wish to take the blessed cure.

In my Spartan cell, I'm shivering. Caught in the primeval battle between the heat and the cold. It is raining tropically and the wind is gusting. The stream behind the rest house has turned into a torrent. The huge rock slabs leading to the summit will be water-slick. Forget completing the climb in this tempest. Could even be snowing on the summit. I wouldn't mind witnessing la neige à Bornéo. But wise Ebin would recommend against pushing on in this downpour. In any case, at Panar Laban, it is cold enough. I've reached my goal.

Belly cramps, bowels threatening havoc. The joys of the tropics. Sipping steaming mee soup and drinking sweet tea to ward off swamp fever at high altitude.

You don't have malaria, mate. You caught a chill. Should have worn your woolly.

Monsieur Hulot? What are you doing here?

Told you. This mountain's my back garden.

I mean. In my room.

The place's full. We have to bunk up together. Rest. I'll take care of you. Reminds me of my dying Sue.

I'm not dying.

So many friends, we had, the world over. For forty years, Hugh and Sue Low on their great walkabout. Going everywhere together. You've heard the phrase, waltz Matilda?

You mean "Waltzing Matilda," don't you?

That's the old bush ballad. To waltz Matilda means to carry a swag. That was us. Carrying a swag and not much else. Quite the team, we were, Hugh and Sue Low. Last year, Hugh lost Sue.

I must be delirious. The struggle between the heat and the cold causing confusion on the brain. And I'm hallucinating. Where did monsieur Hulot misplace Sue Low? Or, more likely, Sue went on a walkabout by herself for some peace and quiet. Sue Low lying low on Low's Peak, waiting for mate man to get lost in the fog, or fall off a cliff, or die of hypothermia. I am shivering. I am delirious.

Your chill's getting worse, mate. Same delirium as with my Sue.

The narrow bed is spinning round and round. I'm dozing on and off, dizzy. Wind howling and rain drumming on the small window pane above my jumping bed. A machete. He's wielding a jungle machete. Will crack open my cranium. He gives an expert whack. It cracks open. The durian stinks up the whole room. Fetid shit smell. Did I make a mess in the bed?

Here. Eat this.

The Australian feeding me my forbidden fruit. Rather pasty, Tiger's favourite. More vegetable than fruit. Flesh, somewhat like soft marrow. Swallowing soft sorrow. The taste reminding me of almond custard. The food of invalids. The smell rising though, closer to a very ripe Roquefort. The complex nature of Borneo imbedded in a durian.

Good jungle tucker, mate, to help your system get rid of your bug.

Monsieur Hulot tucking me in. Wiping my face with a cold cloth.

I grab his wrist: Please, stop harassing me with your kindness.

You're delirious. Sue was too. Don't crack a mental. I'm here. The Natives believe durian makes you sweat.

Sweat! Sweat! The last thing on this planet I want is to sweat.

You're right. There's no scientific basis for this belief other than empirical knowledge. Are you experiencing some of it? Empirical knowledge?

The reputed stink's real enough.

Too right, ratbag! Too right!

I enter fitful sleep. Wind and rain lashing at my brain trigger a roller coaster of dreams. Losing Sab between hotel and airport, Sab reappearing, Sab extracting toxins from the forbidden

durian, Jillanto handcuffed to Mr. Australia dousing himself
with eau de durian, Jillanto and monsieur Hulot, for better or for
worse, in health and in sickness, mates forever.

Feeling better, mate?

Belly cramps are subsiding. Put feet on the floor. Stumble to
my Spartan toilet. Without much ado, wearing only his shorts, a
towel thrown over his shoulder, monsieur Hulot barges in.

I'll be done in a minute, Hugh.

No need to bail out, mate.

He strips, soaps himself *thoroughly* and, using the ubiquitous
hose, sluices himself. I'm no prude, but certain bodily functions
are best performed in private. With ostentation, before turning
off the tap, he drinks from the hose.

No need to boil the water here. Not like in the low-lying areas.
You know why?

Too slow to answer, I must submit to a detailed lecture on the
matter of drinking water in Asia. One has to be on the constant
alert for water-borne nasty diseases, cholera and dysentery being
the most common, until he reveals the great secret of the purity
of water above treeline, as if my Rockies hadn't educated me on
the subject.

After splashing pristine water over my face and neck, I feel
somewhat better. Hungry even. Five P.M. Time for dinner.

In the sparingly furnished restoran, I order karbau steak and
chips. Would enjoy a beer, which is on the menu, brought up
like every other morsel by porters and guides. Decide against.
Less garbage for them to carry back down. Besides, best not to
push my luck and risk getting sick on booze. Among the modest
selection on display, I choose a poskad showing the mountain
in its full sunshine regalia. On the back of the card, I write: Très
chère Sab, wish you were here. Gillo.

Using his knowledge of Malay, monsieur Hulot gets access
to the kitchen. He explains to me that he will prepare himself

a dinkum meal, to honour dear departed Sue who, long ago, convinced him to do away with the unhealthy Aussie barbie (he shakes his head at my karbau steak and chips), in favour of simple oriental fare. He is making himself a mess of vegetables, noodles and rice, followed by a dessert of tiny bananas, which he brought with him. He admits, not as original as carrying a durian up a mountain.

Through the server window, I watch him, as one would an actor on stage. He peels and jabbers, chops and chatters, dices and blabbers. As the vegetables pile up on the chopping board, so do his words; quite mesmerizing. Cooking rice, stir-frying vegetables, the heat, the lack of sanitary installations, cotton pants, anything is a trigger for him to expose at length on his knowledge of Asia. Amazing, to talk so much to say so little. It must be a condition brought on by recent widowhood.

He bangs cupboard doors in search of peanut oil. Finds only palm oil: Oh, no no no no no. Palm oil is absolute chunder. The worst, the very worst.

One tablespoon, monsieur Hulot. Not a whole tankard. One tablespoon won't kill you.

You're young, mate. You can afford to do a perish once in a while. Not me. Oh no no no no no. Now, in these circumstances, the missus, she'd call me a wowser, and would break her own health rule.

Steam the rice for fucksake. I keep grim silence to allow him the pleasure of working the problem for himself. I'm starting to sweat again. The durian effect? It's Ebin's secret, the secret of the two Orang Ulu teksi passengers I want to crack. Dusun and Orang Ulu people, the sweatless ones. Eh, Hugh! Do you sweat? The question never leaves my lips. To ask would be to submit to une réponse interminable. And yet, I must know. The first chance I get, I'll ask Ebin. For now, I'm content to watch monsieur Hulot buzz about, busy busy, a dishtowel rakishly tucked into the waistband of his khaki pants, monsieur Hulot, kitchen boy of the high camp.

While stir-frying his veggies in a wok, he talks about fried rice as breakfast food, which Europeans in hotels all over the island shun in favour of toast and marmalade. To his credit, he did steam the rice. Now, he stirs it with a flourish, leaping to reach for the salt shaker, sprinkling salt from a great height.

In this spectacle, comical on the surface, I am beginning to detect pathos. Although, slapping the man into silence is a more primitive impulse, I can't help but feel pity, une réelle pitié, for his acute loneliness, which is not sweating out of every pore, but borne on the tongue, the way a dog pants to stay cool. Hugh Low's loquacity extraordinaire, a great wail of pain for lost Sue Low.

And I feel a little heartache of my own thinking about Sab and me, separated by heat and jungle, cold rain and high altitude. Could we, like Sue and Hugh, never see each other again? And to think we have acquired the habit of believing that the current of friendship between two people can never run as powerfully as the current of love.

He carries his plateful to the long table where I've been sitting alone, eating karbau and watching him and feeling sorry for myself and my disastrous holiday in these "tristes tropiques." Produces his personal chopsticks. Tucks in. We eat, I in silence and retreat, he talking and chewing without choking. With each bite, he moves himself and his plate closer and closer to me.

Once the food has been dispatched, I sip tea and lime juice, while back in the kitchen, he fusses with the kettle to make himself instant coffee, which he does not usually drink, but there is no tea to his liking in the rest house, the best tea being grown on the slope of... Another endless explanation.

Back in my bare monk cell, I try to sleep under wool blankets. Now that the cold cure is in full swing and that my body

experiences deep in the bone the effect of lack of heat and that
memory has all but forgotten the heat of the jungle, I summon
the spirits of the mountain to summon Sab... The mind stays
suspended on her face in the video, on her face etched in light
and shadow on rock, and I tumble into the blessed sleep cure.

I wake up. One A.M. The wind is still howling, shaking the
shelter in the best chinook tradition, but it has stopped raining.
In the next bed, monsieur Hulot is sawing logs. I glance out
the window. The sky is as clear as in outer space, stars shining
blindingly. I follow the progress of a satellite. On the horizon
are visible the lights of Kota Kinabalu. Far below, the lights of
villages dot the jungle. At this hour, are the Dayak revellers,
high on tuak, giggling and paddling across the molasses river
toward their two-light-bulb village? Where is Sab at this hour?
Returning safely and triumphantly to her jungle bungalow with
a bag full of miraculous plants? Learning from the housekeeper
where I have gone, without pause or refreshment, jumping back
into her jeep, driving on the hairpin highway, headlamp lighting
her way up the mountain trail, setting up at a trot toward the
top, passing me by at Laban Rata, Sab, besting her best climbing
time? I doze off.

Doors are banging.

Two A.M. Still no rain, wind still gusting. And bunk mate
still snoring like a babi boar. Sleep for me will no longer be
an option. And when he wakes up from his slumber, fresh as
a daisy, he will vomit words all over me. My loose bowels have
settled and, although it is cold, I'm no longer shivering.

In the restoran, the half-asleep young servers are wearing
bulky sweaters over their sarongs and the trekkers are brimming
with excitement. I force myself to eat something. Remembering
our hunger when Sab and I trekked to Chinatown in the wee
hours, a fine conclusion to nos folles nuits de Montréal. I drink

sweet tea and nibble on French toast. In the back, his head right
into the kitchen sink, the cook is hawking with such abandon,
it sounds like terminal retching. His dreams must have been
ferocious, for his need to expel much evil spirit is strong. I too
must hawk. Losing Hugh, that lump in my throat, has become
an urgent necessity. As urgent as my need for a cold snap. And
so, to escape one and find the other, I must finish the climb.
And so, I am allowing the call of the cold to lure me where I may
encounter hypothermia.

At three A.M., wearing all my layers of clothing, I join Ebin
outside. He is lightly dressed in fleece pants and a windbreaker
over his hoodie. He still carries no pack. Most likely, he keeps
extra clothing at the rest house, guarded by the spirits of the
mountain. I wonder if they do laundry. Divested of his propane
tank, he seems so light, the fierce wind could transport him to
the summit. No wonder his climbing time is so good. I turn on
my headlamp, he his small torch, and he leads the way. Leaving
the shelter of the balcony, the wind seizes us. I'm surprised by its
warmth.

We begin the climb via a series of rough wooden steps and
scaffoldings anchored to the cliffs, keeping footing and balance
over granite slabs by means of ropes fixed to bolts drilled into
the rock. An easy and mysterious climb in the middle of the
night, une nuit extraordinaire dotted with the flickering lights of
the climbers and their guides following us.

Ebin waits for me: Jillanto, down there, Tamparuli. Village
and river with same name. My home.

Tamparuli. The home of a man. I so wish Sab were here.
Once back down at headquarters, I'll mail her the poskad.
Add that I had a marvellous time in her absence. I do feel her
presence against my shoulder. Spending this night out with Sab
in the high mountains of Borneo, the thick jungle below, lush

with secret plants, above, the stars of the southern hemisphere sharing the sky with the equatorial half moon lying on its back.

Sab, the scientist. I do admire the true scientific mind. Not the operators of the world. Not the prima donnas. Not those who seek an advantage through position of power and through honours only to advance their career. But the true scientific mind that investigates tirelessly. Is curious for the sake of discovering the hidden functions and the minute mechanics of the physical world. And on this steep incline, a new thought forms in my mind. The effect of high altitude? Perhaps, but it seems to me, and without going gaga sentimental about it, that scientists, the true ones, are the only gods. If we must have gods at all.

A little after four, we reach tin shacks fitted with bunk beds and no mattresses, a primitive refuge for a dozen people. At 3,810 metres, Sayat Sayat is nestled next to the 3,932-metre Kinabalu South Peak. We take a fifteen-minute rest in the empty shack. In the other shelter, the group of Malays who spent the night here are sitting on the floor in a circle of candlelight. They are singing, I presume, ancestral incantations to the akis who inhabit Nabalu.

Ebin educates me: These Malays are Christians. They sing hymns to their god. For success on climb and to appease ancestors' spirits.

Wouldn't the dead protect them from mishaps on the mountain?

Ebin doesn't say. I drink from my water bottle, while he energizes himself by chewing betel nuts. I offer him the bottle. He declines: Thank you, no, Jillanto. I don't get thirsty when I climb. I don't sweat.

I say nothing, but I'm damn confounded. Nobody sweats in this land dissolving in humidity!

Not at all, Ebin?

That is so, Jillanto.

I don't buy that, but keep quiet. Despite my empirical knowledge of observing Ebin and the Orang Ulu men, even mate man, everybody sweats. Granted. Sab doesn't sweat much. And granted, I'm the grand champion of the overactive glandes sudoripares. Can't stop rehydrating. I perspire faster than I can replenish fluid, aware of the danger of severe dehydration. Thinking back, I haven't had a decent piddle in days. Seem to piss gold buckshot. Will leave this Borneo paradise a shrunken head. .

So, tell me, Ebin, is it adaptation? A genetic trait acquired over the millennia to keep jungle people from swimming in perpetual sweat? Nevertheless, living in a steamy jungle, if you don't perspire, how do you cool off?

Ebin gets up. Time to go. Four thirty and the night is not so dark anymore. Another two hundred and ninety metres to the summit. We leave Sayat Sayat. The Malays are still chanting, but the elucidation of the source of their music has dulled the enchantment, whereas the mystery of the no-sweat people is kept intact by the betel-nut-chewing guide.

In the greyness of pre-dawn, we are ascending a steep gully leading to the immense summit plateau, composed of gently sloping slabs several hundred metres wide. We pass shadowy outcrops, the higher lesser peaks that form this mighty multi-summit mountain. I tick them off as Ebin names them. Tunku Abdul Rahman at 3,948 metres. The Ugly Sisters at 4,032 metres. Donkey's Ears at 4,054 metres. And the ridge to the mist-shrouded peak called St. Johns at 4,096 metres. The naming coupled with the incremental accumulation of elevation gain in muscle effort and lung capacity give me courage. We are still using our night lights and so are the other climbers, fireflies ascending. We are still in the lead and I am feeling strong.

At five thirty, a glow appears in the eastern sky. Ebin points north to Low's Peak, our destination. For the last couple of hundred metres, we scramble over scree made of large boulders, a terrain I know well, as if the Rockies had answered my call for the cold and transported their distinctive geology to this island to make my feet, twisting in the rubble, feel at home.

At five fifty A.M., we can't climb any higher. We've reached Low's Peak, the highest point on Aki Nabalu. Ebin and Jillanto standing at 4,101 metres above the exotic South China Sea. New satellite imaging will trigger fierce debates challenging or cancelling the claim of the revered place of the dead as the highest peak in the region. Trifles from valley-bound folks. Carry a mountain in your body, regardless of its ranking on some list, and it bears heft and height fully enough. We have summited. I shake hands with my gentle and considerate guide. For such a massive mountain, the summit is tiny. However, it offers a formidable drop on the opposite side from our arrival, the drop guarding the jungle far below.

I express disappointment: The lofty peak of the revered place of the dead, Ebin, should not bear an English name.

In honour of Sir Hugh Low, Jillanto.

Yes, yes, but. Same thing in our Rockies back in Canada. English names all over the place. Why not a tribal name? Do you think others made it to the top before Sir Hugh Low, but didn't boast about it?

Boast?

Officially record the date of their conquest. They always say words like conquest or bag or assault. For all to see and for all times.

That is boast?

Yeah.

Many tribes near mountain. That is so for thousands of years.

Then, it's not unlikely... I see your point. Those Brit adventurers went everywhere. They also tramped all over our

Rockies. They called themselves peak baggers. Preachers too, a
number of them.

Before they reached base of mountain, Jillanto, Sir Hugh Low
and expedition had to hack through jungle for many weeks.

Talk about sweating buckets. No trail?

He did not know where trails were.

That makes me feel better. Let the bastard sweat. In early
morning light, I make out what we have just climbed. Sheer cliffs
drop from the summit plateau on three sides. Peaks appear and
disappear in the mist. Distant hills emerge through layers of
clouds lending an image of islands nestled in the crested waves
of a silver sea. The wind is still blowing strong, the temperature
not much above 5°C. And I am shivering. Not because of a bug,
but with genuine ancient cold.

Soon, our fellow climbers are crowding the narrow summit,
claiming their own personal victory. I crane my neck, expecting
Sab to jog behind the last climber, shouting, surprise, Lanctôt
my man. Surprise!

Dawn rises not pink orange, but in swirls of a thick grey
vapour. Soon, the sunrise paints an array of shades and colours
on the cloud backdrop that stubbornly denies us the much
heralded splendour of the rising sun over the South China Sea.
That change in the pre-arranged program does not prevent a
plethora of photos and grins. I slip on a pair of cotton socks over
my hands to protect them from the cutting icy wind blowing in
this spirit place. If only I could stow away some of that froidure
and carry it back down with me. At six thirty, Ebin motions it is
time to leave the summit.

Can't we stay for a full day cycle?

What for, Jillanto?

I wish to... meditate.

He narrows his eyes: Jillanto not cold enough? We must start
down. Better sweat all your buckets, than have mountain sickness.

I acknowledge. How many weirdos with wacky requests has he guided up here?

On the descent, I'm slip-sliding on the wet rock and, soon, I take a bad spill, landing on my back. Normally, even a daypack would have cushioned my fall. This time, something stabbed me. What the hell did I put in there? Of course. The remains of the durian. I packed it, as I couldn't allow anyone but me to carry the stinker back down. I regret that I did not have the presence of mind to leave it on the summit. An offering of respect to the akis of the mountain for granting me my cold moment. Yesterday in the downpour at Panar Laban, it did not occur to me either to sacrifice the durian to appease the mountain spirits.

Ebin worries. I urge him not to. Imagine my back punctured in a starburst pattern by the sharp spikes of tiger's fruit. My broken skin will fester in the jungle heat and I will develop a deadly infection. Sab will treat it with boiled bark and will tend to my fever with kindness and amusement. The durian and its putrid flesh would only have been trash left on the mountain. We resume the descent, reaching Sayat Sayat quickly.

In spite of holding on to the fixed ropes, I can't stop slipping. My legs—two jellyfish—and my running shoes giving me poor traction. I had figured a vacation in a tropical jungle didn't warrant carrying my hiking boots. We are now traversing one particularly entertaining section with a substantial drop, which darkness on the way up had made inexistent. I go down carefully, mindful of my recent habit of slipping. Ebin perches alertly on the outside, ready to assist me should I lose my footing. I appreciate he who is guiding me so safely and skilfully, but, considering the difference in our sizes, should I begin to slide, I would take him down with me. May the spirits of the dead forgive my arrogance for seeking cold at near zero degrees of latitude where it has no true lease.

In ninety minutes of my not very graceful descent, we are
back at Laban Rata where I drink large quantities of Sabah tea.
Monsieur Hulot-mate is nowhere in sight.

From then on, everything goes fast, as if we had entered
a race. At eight forty-five, we resume the hike down through
thickening vegetation and toward increasing heat. I keep looking
back, caught in a powerful urge to rush back up on jellyfish legs,
my ears filled with the beguiling high notes of the near-freezing
wind of dawn. Instead, my nose is now filling with the repulsive
odour of the decaying flesh of the fruit, which has saturated
pack, clothing, skin, my very breath. Dripping wet in the jungle
steamer, I exude the fine scent of eau de raw sewage.

On the forested path, my knees and quads can't take it
anymore. Ebin fetches me a branch to use as a walking stick.
The path is slick with mud churned in yesterday's rains. I slide
and stumble on the rocks strewn along it. Each time I find
myself on my ass, Ebin goes tut-tut-tut, a teacher reproaching
his undisciplined student. That is moi in the flesh, the lazy
pupil with his head in the clouds and his ass in the mud. As we
descend, the dreaded sticky heat of the jungle wraps around my
body its multiple arms covered in suckers. And with decreasing
altitude and increasing heat, the stink of the durian gains in
potency. Quietly, Ebin puts more and more distance between us.

It is high noon when we reach headquarters, after
descending, from summit to power station, 2,272 metres.
Even on level ground, I am unable to support my weight. A
disarticulated puppet, I bid Ebin goodbye with many thanks.
With regrets that we didn't linger in the frigidarium of the
mountain.

At the counter, I receive a certificate of excellence for having
climbed Mount Kinabalu. Grin at the sweet touch. Imagine Parks
Canada handing out certificates to all successful peak baggers

of Mount Robson. I buy a stamp and drop the poskad into the mailbox by the door. Someone says the bas will soon depart for Kota Kinabalu. My port of exit. And home. Will the bas wait, the last available seat permanently reserved for Jillanto? I rush to grab my large pack left in storage. Exit into the brutal sun.

Begging your pardon, ratbag. You stink to high hell.

This, mate, is the empirical knowledge of durian.

Going back down?

Nah. I've had it with the green inferno. Though, I have a cool friend living down there. Dr. Gustavia Sabourin. She's an alchemist sorcerer, that one. She could give me a root, a rhizome, a leaf, a seed. Any concoction from her herbal cornucopia to cure swollen sweat glands and to curb this unbearable sweating of mine. To say nothing of healing punctures by durian.

If you change your mind, here's a parting gift from your mate.

And he hands me a tube of potent Aussie-made insect repellent.

It may dissolve plastic, but it's guaranteed to resist removal caused even by your excessive sweating. It'll keep you safe from all those bugs out there. And that's dinkum talk from your mate. Well, it was a challenge spending time in your company. A bit of advice. Don't be so stroppy. Learn to slow down. You'll enjoy the tropics more.

On that note, he gets on the bas, taking the last available seat. Leans out the open window.

My Sue was trigger-happy. She'd still be alive if she hadn't been so frazzled all the time. So, mate, don't fight it. Welcome yourself to paradise.

▲ Squeaky clean after a long shower, I take a later bas driving down Aki Nabalu. Toward the sea, toward the jungle.

I write Sab another poskad: I'm not staying, old pal. With the sunrise, I'm outta your Borneo paradise. Must escape this heat that rumbles, steams blood, pops lungs. Must run away from ear-splitting night ménagerie in sticky jungle. Midnight monkeys moaning in monotone. Nocturnal parrots mimicking rusty hinges. Two o'clock tuak-carousing Dayaks paddling splat. Dogs snarling. Night barge roaring down molasses river. Four o'clock cocks crowing crazy. And the cherry on the ais krim, high-pitched *Anopheles* drilling malaria into skin, into blood. Such is your paradise, Sab, my dearest friend, with its touch of inferno. Not for me. Not for me. Avec toute mon affection from our northern country, your old pal Gillo.

Then, I stare at the tube of insect repellent. Hugh Low's voice in my ear, grating: Don't be so stroppy. Learn to slow down. You'll enjoy the tropics more.

Driving back toward Sab's jungle bungalow. Showing up, smeared with a miracle of chemistry that will keep *Anopheles* at bay. The housekeeper will assure me the doctor is now back from collecting. The extinct plant may or may not be extinct, the expedition, a wild goose chase or a stunning discovery. Sab and I will sit in those big chairs on the veranda. Will sip gin pahits. Will watch the molasses river *flow* by. Will yak up a storm. Slowly reconnecting. While I wait for the inaugural bout of malaria the down-under man swears I haven't got. Jungle fever forever. I am here. Might as well stay a while. Sab, cool as ever. Sab, the healer, will block the signalling pathway of pain, won't she? And when sweating like a babi, I could always hike back up Gunung Kinabalu and find salvation in the realm of the cold. Sweat your buckets, Jillanto. Don't fight it, mate. No sweat, I will tell Sab. No sweat. And Sab sipping her gin pahit will say, Lanctôt my man, so glad you could come. And in this manner, I will welcome myself to your paradise. Because, Sab, old friend, you always got me.

Onion

BAREFOOT, Jacques Lachance staggers into the kitchen, awakened by Maddie's nocturnal activity.

I had no idea, ma grande. It's not just trouble sleeping. You are a true night owl.

Ha! Maddie guffaws, raising her head from her kitchen lab book. I'm nothing but. She taps the book with her pen: Water boils four degrees Celsius lower here in Calgary than in Montréal. Did you know that?

Jacques slips his rock shoes on and, with his chin, points at the display of postcards pinned on the walls and the high ceiling of his Bowness bungalow. He moves his head this way and that, like a bird on a spring: I'm surprised your mom didn't write you about that.

Maddie could not be more surprised than him. A few minutes before, her expectation of success had run high. Now, her first Calgary experiment lies in ruins on the kitchen counter. A few minutes back, the water had come to a full boil. Maddie rinsed the batch of pearl onions that had been steeping in its salt-water basin for two days (200 grams of salt dissolved in two litres of water, she had noted in her book) and dipped them into the stockpot, a few at a time so as not to lower the temperature too much.

When the water boiled again, she counted sixty seconds. Removed the pearls with her skimmer, plunged them into cold water to prevent further cooking. Popped one onion into her mouth. A tad too crunchy. But a tad was a tad. How could that be?

In Montréal, through trial and error in the course of countless sleepless nights, she had taught herself to blanch and skin; steep; dip, count, retrieve, bite. Once she had discovered the perfect equilibrium between cocktail onion size and cooking time, the first three steps of the experiment never failed. Her lab book testifies to that. It was in the final two steps, pickling, then the maturing period, that she kept missing the mark. Were the spices in the pickling solution the problem? Was it better to put them directly into the jar with the cooked onions? Too many spices? Not enough? Chili pepper, ginger root, cinnamon stick, peppercorns, whole cloves, allspice. She tried all permutations. She flipped through the pages of her lab book to study the tables she had made. No matter what, in the final taste test, an unknown factor kept upsetting the balance.

Ultimately, she convinced herself the water was what had ruined them. She would never reach pearl perfection. And here, in Jacques Lachance's house, where she expected to solve the remaining puzzle, her onions remained undercooked. What caused the experiment to fail? She blinked into the blackness of the east window. Had to figure this out.

She boiled fresh water and immersed her candy thermometer. Aha! In school, she had been told, water boils at one hundred degrees centigrade. Her teacher had failed to add, at sea level. And so, here in the shadow of the mountains, water boils at 96°C. No wonder her onions came out crunchier than Mom's, and a tad crunchier than her own dozens of batches in Montréal. Lower temperature means she must leave the bulbs in longer. But how much longer? Calculations of perfect crunchiness or not, she just ruined her first batch of Calgary pickled pearls.

When her mother sent Maddie across the continent, in praise of the water, she meant not the water coming out of the tap, but glacier water. Maddie was willing to learn mountaineering for the sole purpose of fetching it, vital to the success of her experiment. Instead, she met Jacques Lachance, a bona fide climber, and a sweet man, who offered to bring her the precious water from the heights. However, since hauling it is hazardous to him and since he can carry only a limited quantity with each outing, she must use the water wisely. And so, she must solve the problem of the missing four degrees, which she must make up with the exact extra numbers of seconds, and according to the size of her pearl *cepa*. Despite staring at the white light above the stove, she is still groping in the dark.

Jacques finishes lacing his rock shoes and, with great precision, climbs the perimeter walls of his Bowness bungalow. Maddie follows his progress along the open-plan house, all inner walls knocked down, Jacques having turned his home into one big climbing gym. With fingers and toes, he grips plastic holds of various shapes and sizes that, he explained to her, he had bolted to the studs behind the wood panels.

Very safe. You should try it. I'd belay you.

Maybe she will. Watching his ease sharpens her desire.

He rests on his big toes, looking at her: Think about it. Montréal lies pretty close to sea level. Only Mount Royal gives the city some elevation. Its highest point being at a mighty 233 metres.

How do you know that?

I'm a climber. And, like your Mama, something of a bookworm.

She can see that. Books strewn about the place like so many dirty socks.

Calgary, on the other hand, has an elevation of about 1,000 metres.

He climbs sideways as well as up. Like an ant following a beam, he works his way along the slanting ceiling with the special overhangs. Stops and rests on bones, with arms and legs straight. The higher you climb in the mountains, he continues, the lower the atmospheric pressure, the thinner the air and the lower the boiling point of water. Which means that cooking food in high mountains is a major pain in the butt.

He downclimbs, working sideways and, without touching ground, climbs back up, clinging to walls in the front, then to walls in the back of the house. Back up near the ceiling once more, he stops again, locking knees and elbows, twisting his neck to look at her from high above, and grins: If at sea level you made a relish of onions, Maddie baby, and it had to cook for one hour, at 7,000 metres with the water boiling point being 80°C, your relish would take thirteen hours to come out just right. He holds himself in the static position of the monkey hang to strengthen finger tendons, forearm muscles, legs, improve stamina. And, to pass the time, he reads Maddie one of her mom's postcards, which he fixed to the ceiling just the other day:

Père Marquette, ma chérie, staved off hunger when he explored the south shore of Lake Michigan by eating a wild onion (or was it wild garlic?) the Indians in the region called shikaakwa. And this became chicagou to the French explorers.

He moves again and shouts: Isn't that a hoot? Chicago, the Big Onion. Or is it, the Big Garlic?

Amused by his banter, Maddie watches Jacques's reflection in the north window. Feet apart, knees bent, arms fully extended, grabbing the holds above his head, he straightens his legs, now his hands at shoulder level. As he gets up, he reaches with his right hand to a higher hold, then does the same with the other hand and resumes his climbing. He breathes hard, but

otherwise climbs as if walking on the floor. Maddie's onion
practice is as good as Jacques's climbing skills. Why does she
keep peeling off?

Jacques finally lowers himself to the floor and hugs her from
behind, his strong arms warm against her skin. He rubs his body
against the full of her back: Come to bed.

As you just discovered, Jacques, I'm a night owl. My nocturnal
activity will deprive you of sleep. I should move out.

You just moved in. Stay as long as you want and, as promised,
each time I go into the hills, I'll bring you a couple of litres of
glacier water.

She hugs him for his kindness: Jacko, I know how sleep
deprivation can lead to spatial distortion. And in your job as a
roofer and then your climbing, spatial distortion can be fatal.

I can sleep anywhere, my onion lady.

Several more hours of winter darkness will certainly keep
Maddie awake. She will count onions, smell them, watch them
tumble down on the dark panes of the western and southern
windows until the rising sun opens a vista in the east window.
Summer nights have the grace of shortness. She longs for them.

If my noise and the light don't disturb you, the onion
smell will.

I'll get used to your night cookery.

Will he though?

▲ Onion smell. Then, at the kitchen counter, two-year-old
Maddie pressed so hard she pinned Mom's arm down, so that
Mom had to wave her other elbow, as a bird with a broken wing
might use the good wing to save herself. With her free arm, Mom
pushed her out of harm's way of knives and boiling water.

Mais, maman, je veux voir. I want to smell the onion.

At age two, Maddie spoke clearly. Bilingual clearly.

Elle parle franc, proud Papa told Mom.

Whether in mother tongue or dans la langue paternelle, specialized words such as pungent / piquant did not yet exist for little Maddie. So, at her mother's pinned elbow, the child sniffed the unnamed dispersion. How to transform pungent / piquant through the olfactory factory? Later, she thought the word faulty. She refused to associate onions and their allies with the notion of something harmful that presumed to irritate, to sting, to bite. Pungent. The smell connected not with pain, but with desire. Piquant. The sharpness of desire. Nobody would understand, so, quietly, she went in search of the absolute answer. It began with insomnia.

▲ The last time Maddie slept without oblivion interruptus was on her twenty-first birthday. The next day, insomnia began. She had just moved out of Mom's house into a studio apartment on the edge of downtown where the rents were cheaper and paint chipped freely. The floor near the small kitchen counter was so warped she fancied she lived in the crow's nest of an ancient ship. Each time a truck rumbled by, the entire structure swayed. Rats scurried and scratched in the inner walls. At first, she thought it was the rats' scratching that woke her in the indecent hours before sunrise. Her brain spent several nights scurrying on its own in the noisy darkness before it determined what had really woken her.

She smelled onions. Not her neighbours' cooking, not the diner's frying across the street. What she smelled belonged to the earth, to kitchen gardens in the morning. If she had pressed the juice from freshly snapped leek leaves, the damp sand still clinging to them, the scent could not have been sweeter. She sniffed inside the cabinet under the kitchen sink where she kept her onions in an open shoebox. They were dry as they should be and no rat had pierced the layers of crackly skin to get at the juicy flesh.

Maddie discussed the matter with her mother. A few days later, she received this postcard:

Last Saturday, I checked the library, ma chérie. I found no record that rats eat onions, nor, if in times of famine and infestation, rats ruined onion crops, even in the Middle Ages, the golden age of the rat. What I found is that aphids avoid garlic. If one day you have a garden, plant garlic heads among your herbs and edible flowers. I speculate that if aphids are repelled by the sulphur compounds released as they suck the juice of garlic shoots, rats may have developed the same aversion to Allium cepa. *Still, beware. Onions have their pests.*

Maddie pinned Mom's postcard to the wall with a thumbtack.

The rats kept to themselves inside the walls. Still, every night around three A.M., onion vapours swirling inside her nose roused her. She visualized a yellow mist churning in the nasal cavity, snaking through narrow passages opening into the spongy swamp of her brain until the alliaceous mist hit the olfactory bulb. In full smell mode, she closed her eyes, but insomnia took root.

Dizzy chill in the vertigo of night. A distinct constriction of the spine in the caudal region. Sweat, spasms. Legs jerking. Skin itching. Keeping eyes closed. Tumbling into a shallow hole. Heart jumping, strangling the larynx. Constriction in the tail end and no dawn yet. No dawn.

Only that onion smell. Raw, fried, pickled. Mostly pickled. Garlic, shallot, leek, chive, scallion, onion. Mostly pearl onion. Sweet and sour scent, the three o'clock breath. Tart and sweet lacing around the tongue, inside the nose.

Roaming the small room with the warped floor. Listening to rats inside their secret world. The room in darkness hid its ugly face. A yellow glow came in from street lights. Maddie stood at the curtainless window. Grime on glass diffusing the pale light made a curtain of sorts. The street below so deserted, not even alley cats roamed. Outside, through the pearlescent dirt clinging to the window, Maddie saw onions falling from the sky, a hail of pearls pounding the street.

The perversion of making coffee in the middle of insomnia. Strong, black. At three A.M., the jolt in the mouth. Overdosing on insomnia.

Hypnotized, she drew a taste not yet known. Drawing concentric circles on a peeling wall. The transparent, moist skins between the close coats of onion flesh. Outer layers of parchment paper, crisp. Drawing concentric circles. The universe contained in an onion. Onion rings, the fabrication of time.

Later, Mom sent this postcard:

"Indeed the tears live in an onion that should water this sorrow." I am deep into Shakespeare, ma chérie. You are not alone with onion eyes. Try to sleep. Did you drink warm milk with honey and anise seeds and a little grating of nutmeg? Or you may chew on cardamom seeds. The Indonesians recommend cardamom for stomach disturbances which, as you know, can upset the sleep of the most placid person. At the very least, since, as your papa used to say, les oignons font pleurer, you may cry yourself to sleep. Sweet dreams, Daughter.

What about the Lady of Shalott? Did she have dragon breath? Did she cry herself to sleep? Did the sulphurous emanations of her flesh drive her to social distraction? But her beauty was also the mother-of-pearl of the earth in subtle shades of white, yellow and red, mauve, grey, purple and violet. Something not yet occurred formed in Maddie's mind.

Later, Mom sent this postcard:

That diplomat Prior wrote: "Who would ask for her opinion /
Between an oyster and an onion?"

Still drawing concentric circles on walls in the middle of
warped insomnia. Leek / poireau. Investigating the root of the
matter. Kalonji. The black seed of the wild onion. Kali for black
humour? Kalonji, the black seed sprouting out of lidless vigil,
forming concentric circles on walls. Getting hypnotized, getting
closer.

At four A.M., Maddie made Japanese rice that she seasoned
with powdered green tea and rice vinegar. She smelled the rice.
Mild, sweet. A pearl onion flitted across her mind, a shadow on
her night walls of concentric circles. She formed small sticky balls
between oiled palms and stacked them in a pyramid on a glass
plate. The rice balls released a faint pickled onion smell and they
did resemble cocktail onions. After her nuits blanches, her stomach
quivered. Even cardamom seeds wouldn't help. She could only
eat the gentle grain, sacred in other parts of the world where
people slept. And she catnapped in the corners of certain hours.

For twelve nights, the smell of onion followed her everywhere.

She roamed the streets; the smell accompanied her. She
tensed up at noises hiding in shadows; the smell clung to her.
On her way back to her room, she passed under the purple
neon sign of a martini glass with a swizzle stick of light and an
olive at the bottom of the glass. The purple had a defect and the
olive shone white. Not a martini then; rather, a Gibson. She saw
herself snatch the pearl. Pop it into her mouth.

At five A.M. on the twelfth night, out of the irritant of sleep
deprivation, she knew she had to create the perfection of a
thousand-year-old pearl.

▲ Maddie visited her mother's house.

Mom, I have a calling. Le sacerdoce de l'oignon.

Le sacerdoce de l'oignon? Sounds serious.

It is. I can't sleep. I smell onions all night long. Be my mentor. Teach me everything you know about onions.

Lillian was halfway through *Bouvard et Pécuchet*. She laid the book face down on her lap and motioned her daughter to sit on the ottoman. Maddie plopped herself down at Mom's feet, waiting for her to reveal the secrets of *Allium cepa*.

Madeleine, you could be having brain seizures. Those recurring smells worry me. Onion is likely related to childhood memory. A mother–daughter bonding over a basin of cocktail onions and boiling vinegar and sugar. Do you smell spices as well? You don't? I may have added a pinch of ginger, but I don't think so. In my day, clove and ginger were reserved for the Christmas tourtières, and cinnamon for the autumn apple pies. But that persistent phantom smell of onion. Did my pickling activities traumatize you? It would be wise to see a neurologist and asked for a CAT scan.

Lillian gripped the spine of *Bouvard et Pécuchet*.

But, Mom, why presume the worst? I want to know everything there is to know about onions. And my dream. Shall I tell you my dream? My dream is to make the perfect pickled onions. Cocktail onions that will send the eater into fits of ecstasy. I want to make the pearl onion queen of aphrodisiacs.

Ovid thought the white shallot from Megara was an aphrodisiac.

Will you teach me, Mom? Will you?

Lillian tapped the cover of *Bouvard et Pécuchet* with her forefinger: Ces messieurs failed miserably in their attempt at canning. Mould and mildew in every jar. You will not, I hope, throw yourself lightly into canning. As you know, since your papa's stomach took him away from us, I have no desire to go back to the kitchen. I padlocked it, remember. Of course, I still make myself BLTS and cups of tea. But nothing beyond the simplest food. Besides, let's face it. My pickled onions were of the humblest fare, in the tradition of our farming grandmothers. Unlike you, I had no calling. So, my empirical knowledge will be of little use to you. Lillian reopened *Bouvard et Pécuchet*: This is where I dine now, Madeleine. I tell you what. Experiment. Meanwhile, if in my readings I come across something useful to your search, I'll pass it on to you.

But Mom, you learned at your mother's elbow. And she at her mother's elbow.

Lillian flapped one elbow and laughed: So did you, ma chérie. So did you. That smell of onions is the surest path to your deep memories of the early kitchen. Follow your nose. It will guide you. I will help you through my readings, but not the other way.

Will you worry about brain seizures?

I won't force you to apply poultices to your forehead.

With Mom's blessing, Maddie hiked the onion trail, sometimes over steep bends, sometimes along sweet alliaceous stretches. Always guided by desire. The trail brought her far from her early Montréal memories. Failed to cure her insomnia, but filled her slanted Montréal flat with information on the ancient *Allium* family.

Shortly after her visit to Mom's house, Maddie received a postcard that had nothing to do with onions:

I came across the distant cousin of your thousand-year-old pearl, ma chérie. The Chinese thousand-year egg. In a wooden bowl, clay is mixed with lime, ashes, salt and black tea leaves. Rice husks are crushed into the mush. An uncooked duck egg is coated with the material and buried in a clay pot for three

months. Such a descent into darkness may appear to take
forever, say, one thousand years. In its anaerobic environment
and with a little underground heat, the egg white becomes
firm, amber-coloured and transparent like jelly. Sometimes
with feathery markings. The yolk turns dark green and becomes
firm without losing its moisture. One never gobbles up paydon
the way one does a pickled egg at a fish-and-chip shop counter
after pub-closing time. Rather, a morsel is served as an appetizer
on a toothpick with a slice of ginger. A fitting tribute, following
the delicacy of unearthing, removing husk and clay, peeling
and slicing the egg. Revealing the work of time and darkness
and seclusion. Can your cocktail onion surpass paydon,
Madeleine?

▲ Cleaning the mess of the failed first Calgary experiment,
Maddie turns to Jacques.

I had to take up Mom's challenge. Her challenge was as
pungent as onion smell. Tout aussi piquant. It piqued my
curiosity. It was as enticing, if you know what I mean, as the
sharpness of desire.

I understand that, the sharpness of desire.

Ah, oui?

Certainly. It's all there in mountain climbing. If I tell you
about the excitement and the frustration and the challenge and
the many repeats of a hard route through all kinds of weather
until you finish it, and then, what a relief, what a release, you will
understand that I understand.

I do.

Yes, you do. But until you come along, it'll remain something
of an abstraction. Once you're there, right there in the doing
and the exertion, and in the impatience and the momentum,
only then will you know that I know about that kind of desire.
Mountaineering and the perfect pickled onion you seek. Same

thing. It's not always grand, but it's always worth the trouble. Even its tedious moments...

Tedious! As in peeling a kilo of tiny onions? That, I understand.

And as in your onion practice of peeling and steeping and boiling and pickling, mountaineering may look like you keep doing the same thing over and over. A scree is a scree. A rock face is a rock face. Or ice is ice. Or terror is sheer terror, yeah. But it's not. Each time, it's different. Each and every time, you can taste and smell the sharpness of your desire.

Maddie is astounded. In an odd way and right there in the middle of their Bowness night, just like that, Jacques understands the essentials of onions without ever having pickled a single one. At least, he does, in a kind of abstraction. She turns off the lights and they go to bed. He falls asleep instantly. She, though... Her mind's eye roams the room, searches the myriad maternal postcards that dot the walls of this house.

▲ In rapid succession, Mom's postcards fell into Maddie's Montréal mailbox, bringing her on the Grand Onion Tour:

To Ashkelon you go, ma chérie, the land of the scallion and the shallot. To Egypt, the land of onion worshippers. To Wales, the land of leek patriots. To Chicago, the land of the wild onion (or wild garlic). To Georgia, the land of the Vidalia, sweet as a harvest apple. To Korea, the land of the garlic eaters. To India, the land where five pounds of onions may routinely be cooked down to their essence in lamb korma, the finished concoction filling a bowl no bigger than the hors d'oeuvre dish in which I served my pedestrian cocktail onions.

Maddie thumbtacked to her drab walls Mom's stories gathered along the *Allium* trail of time and places. And still, she did not sleep. And still, each experiment ended in failure.

Beside her, Jacques sleeps, his breath a little urgent. Is he climbing hard rock? Risking rotten ice? Slipping and sliding up tedious scree? She rests the flat of her hand on the small of his back.

One year to the day since the first nuit blanche. And in her hometown, the scurrying in the inner walls seemed to intensify, the floor seemed to warp in an endless wavy motion that gave her le mal de mer. Unless it was sleep deprivation that caused nausea.

On another insomniac nuit montréalaise, still experimenting and failing, kilos of pearls ruined in her attempt to achieve the perfect state of crunchiness, the correct balance between tart and sweet, her onions too perfumed with ginger root or too aggressive with peppercorns, Maddie detected a new anomaly. On that night, following the one-month maturing period, when she twisted open the lid of the jar, her pearls had a persistent, if subtle, taste and smell reminiscent of inferno. Where in hell did the sulphur compounds emanate from?

Maddie read again the postcard thumbtacked above the stove and which Mom had sent a few weeks earlier:

In garlic, once the cell membrane separating the molecule alliin and the enzyme alliinase is cut, the enzyme destroys the unstable alliin molecule to generate another sulphur compound, and this is what imparts the characteristic garlic smell. In the case of onions, a similar process makes you cry, ma chérie. But, there is hope. Since that molecule is water soluble, you will keep dry eyes if you chop under water. Most people don't go to the extreme of diving to chop, but some people go to the extreme of wearing goggles. Or chewing on a hunk of bread. A burned match does not work. Contact lenses, I'm told, do. Though beware of onion myths.

But Maddie's pearls were never cleaved. So, no release of
the lachrymator. And their salt bath and their sixty seconds in
boiling water had never triggered malodorous emanations. The
remaining problem was the ratio of vinegar to sugar, not the
scent of hell. She was at a new crossroads and at a loss. Maddie
continued to read, moving along her walls, letting her too-wide-
open eyes dart among Mom's postcards:

Allium cepa *contains 91% water. Has twenty-eight calories
per 100 grams. Germinates between 9 and 30°C. Tolerates
frosts to –2.5°C. Matures in 115–135 days. The milder the
climate, the milder the* cepa.

Maddie began to speak to her postcards: Ninety-one per
cent water. *Allium*, you are a fine desert food. Low in calories,
you won't send the traveller into fits of night sweats and your
water will keep the pilgrim cool. Toi, l'oignon, tu es la gourde
du désert. Water. Is water the culprit? It's Montréal water, she
declared louder, staggering in her flat-ship anchored on the edge
of downtown.

Montréal water gushing from the tap would not poison. On
the other hand, a faint unpleasant odour, undetectable to the
average city dweller, but noticeable to the sensitive nose of the
chronic insomniac, may have laced the clear liquid. Maddie
noted in her lab book that, either during the two-day steeping in
their cold salt bath or during the crucial minute in their boiling
water bath, her baby onions soaked up the volatile compounds,
which infested them to the core during the one-month maturing
period. Or was the taste, like the onion smell, only in her head?
Mom worried about phantom smells. For that matter, were there
truly rats scurrying in her inner walls?

In the end, the *Allium* trail brought Maddie to Calgary via the
waterway and, possibly, to onion salvation. Jacques is sleeping

now, in the fetal position, his breathing calm. In the dark, Maddie's mind reads Mom's last Montréal postcard:

It is worth going, Madeleine, if only for the water. And the City by the Bow being rat-free, you may finally sleep. I read in a travel book that the Calgary water is nonpareil, coming deep from the frozen land in high mountains west of the city. As good beer begins with pure spring water, I surmise that glacier water will give genius to the genus and only then will you achieve the perfect pickled onion. Or, as you baptized it, your thousand-year-old pearl, for which, like its counterpart, the preserved egg, some period of burial must be accepted. When you achieve success, send me a jar. As your papa used to say, bonne chance, ma fille.

▲ Back in Montréal, Maddie stored her postcards and thumbtacks in a plastic box. The pasty walls with the peeling paint appeared pockmarked. With a felt pen, she connected the thumbtack holes at random. Stepped back from her drawing as far as the cramped room allowed. To the vivid imagination or sleep-deprived eyes, the lines formed a giant head of garlic, with the skinny tails of rats scurrying away in terror of *Allium sativum*.

Maddie stuffed her few possessions in a backpack. Invited Mom to a farewell dinner in a bistro on rue Saint-Denis.

Lillian declined: This month, I'm banqueting with Proust, ma chérie. But I promise to write.

Maddie watched Montréal grow smaller under the belly of the plane.

Later a flight attendant shook her until she woke up. They had landed in Calgary twenty minutes before.

And here she is in Jacques's bed. His sleep seems agitated again. Is he falling off a ledge? Is the smell of onion attacking his brain deep in his slumber? She warned him. He dismissed her warning. She should leave his house. Why torment him with the pungency of her desire? The sharpness of his own should suffice. Sooner or later, he will kick her and her onion obsession out, so he may sleep in peace.

▲ After the flight attendant kicked her out of her seat and Maddie deplaned, she stayed at the Y while drumming up business as a window dresser. As soon as she could afford to, she would move into a place of her own and resume her *Allium cepa* experiments.

One day in early December, Maddie was dressing the window of a high-end jewellery and glassware store on 17th Avenue. She dropped white glass pearls into martini glasses she had filled with water and glycerine to enhance their size. Added coloured glass swizzle sticks. Then arranged her display on draped white satin. She was finishing her composition with a river of pearls cascading from empty, tipped glasses when she felt watched. From the corner of her eye, she caught sight of a young man with thick black hair sticking straight out of his skull, wearing a red Gore-Tex jacket, black fleece pants and steel-toed work boots. Before she could give him a look of annoyance, he raised his hand and formed the O of approval with thumb and forefinger. Her face relaxed into a smile and, immediately, he pointed at the martini glasses and, taking the pose of a swell in a film noir, mimicked drinking cocktails together. She nodded and motioned, wait a moment.

At The Martini Bar, she insisted on buying the first round: Let's have Gibsons.

Gibsons? At a *martini* bar?

They're interesting to me, and they're cousins. Apparently, the Gibson was named after a teetotalling American ambassador of the Prohibition era. At functions, for diplomacy's sake, he had to drink with his guests. So, he carried water in a martini glass to which he added a cocktail onion. And today's Gibson is just a dry martini with an onion. Perfect for martini bars.

They toasted their encounter. Sipping his drink, he watched her perform a new slant on the old come-on. Between her fingernails, she daintily seized the pearl at the bottom of her glass. Inhaled the sweet-tart scent. Rolled the bulb between thumb and index finger. With eyes half-closed, she licked it, the tip on her tongue hard against the white flesh. Wrapped her lips around the onion, parted her teeth and sucked it into her mouth, rolling it from side to side, then bit. He imagined vinegar and sugar exploding in droplets of sharpness and softness on her tongue and rising in vapour up her nasal cavity to lodge deep inside her brain, causing her whole body to arch, her skin to shiver. She swallowed and opened her eyes.

He sipped his gin: Was it good for you? He couldn't begin to imagine what she could do with a gherkin.

She drained her glass, shaking her head: Complete imbalance of sugar and vinegar. And cheap vinegar too. French wine vinaigre is best, but it costs an arm and a leg.

She leaned so close to his face he smelled her onion breath, and wanted to kiss her.

She licked her lips: Ultimately, the secret is the water. That's why I came to Calgary. My mother, who is an expert, told me if I use glacier water, I'll make the perfect pickled pearl. The problem is, how do you get to the glaciers? We're not talking ice cubes from the freezer tray. Nevertheless, the water brought me to Calgary. What brought you here? Veux-tu qu'on parle français?

Non non. Anglais is fine. I have one of each.

One of each what?

Parents. Ma mère est une Anglo. Mon père est un Franco.

Moi aussi! Same configuration. How about that! My name is Zoé Madeleine Rivière. Everybody calls me Maddie.

He laughed, rubbing his steely hair: My name is Jacques Lachance. Everybody calls me Jack Lastchance. I came here for the climbing.

Maddie's eyes sparkled: You're kidding me.

Why would a guy called Jack Lastchance kid you? You've seen the Rocks. They're but a stone's throw away from the city. I can tell you about glaciers. Teach you climbing techniques. On rock, ice. The lot.

She insisted on buying the second round.

I may not know my pearl onion from a gherkin, but I can recognize the right woman when she comes along.

He invited Maddie to move her bags from the Y to his Bowness bungalow, which he had been renovating forever and was in no hurry to finish.

When not shingling roofs, I climb. If you're not ready just yet, on my way back from the mountains, I can bring you a small supply of glacier water.

The second round of Gibsons arrived and they toasted their new venture.

Maddie observed him. He seemed like un bon gars and his offer was irresistible.

Jacques, my very own porteur d'eau. Oh, I don't mean in the old contemptuous appellation of hewers of trees and carriers of water. You will carry glacier water in triumph.

That same evening in early December, she hung up her stockpot and canner and jars and skimmer and kitchen scale and measuring cups, the tools of her search, on whatever sections of the walls not taken by Jacques's climbing gear. The house was bare, except for a few pieces of furniture and stacks of books. Mom would approve of this roofer-climber-bookworm.

As for Maddie, she delighted in the large windows facing the four points of the compass, especially the ones looking south and west at the mountains and the big sky. She could grow chives and scallions and, perhaps, leeks in boxes. Jacques had no problem with verdure in the house. He helped her with her collection of postcards. When they ran out of walls, he climbed and fixed the cards to the ceiling. He downclimbed and carried her to his bed.

▲ Now that Maddie is settled in Jacques Lachance's Bowness bungalow, she daydreams of successful pickling days, while Jacques never misses his chance to go to the mountains with one of his several climbing buddies. Maddie has yet to buy hiking boots and crampons and a harness and a helmet.

Jacques raises his hands: No pressure, ma grande.

And he leaves, excited-expectant. And he comes back, exhausted-elated. Pumped, he tells her. His mouth frothing with tales of spindrift and bergschrund, rock pelting him and his partner, postholing in knee-deep snow, crevasse rescue, a close call inches from an avalanche, a seven-pitch climb on beautiful plastic ice; tales of wondrous days. Tales, it seems to Maddie, extracted from the ancient myths of Coyote the Trickster or Raven the Messenger, rock and ice, mountain spirits with a mind of their own. And Jacques and his climbing partners, mere mortals, battling the Eternal Elements. Does her onion obsession seem as unreal to him as this climbing thing appears to her?

Outrageous, Jacques, what you do. Simply outrageous. Will I ever be ready to try this climbing of yours for myself?

He turns the stained pages of her lab book, stares at graphs, then at drawings of *Allium*. Grins at her: I'm curious about this stuff you're doing. But, no pressure.

In between going out and coming back, Maddie loses sight of him, having no clue (not really) what he could be doing out there and how. But each time, he comes back with his bag full of astounding tales and with a few litres of glacier water. Maddie tastes the water and, soon, she can identify the glacier from which Jacques drew it. She claims she can tell the difference between the water from the Rae, or the Bow, or the Victoria, or the Athabasca.

Until they all melt, ma grande, an endless parade of glaciers to choose from.

Maddie inspects the water from the Athabasca: I don't know, Jacques. But visiteurs' feet dirtying the toe of the glacier will ruin my pearls. I admit to having a soft spot for the Bow Glacier.

I get the water way higher than any tourist goes. Only your imagination, not the water, alters the taste of your onions. I bet this tap water, which by the way comes from the Bow Glacier, would do just fine.

Yes, but this tap water's been treated. Are you saying I don't know my onions?

I don't mind carrying water from any glacier, Madeleine, but don't push it. You must accept what I bring you. I carry lots of gear. I can't hop from glacier to glacier...

Okay, okay. I'll be out of here in a jiffy. I told you you'd end up kicking me...

Relax. I'm not kicking you and your onions out.

You don't look like you mean it.

I'm bushed. But what I mean is this. When you begin exploring glaciers yourself, you can take your pick and be your own water carrier. Until then... Now, you mind bailing from this pointless argument?

You're right, Jacques. This is dumb. Nitpicking about glacier water. Still, I swear the Athabasca does something not quite right to my pearls.

What? What is it the Athabasca does to your pearls?

She can't tell. Perhaps insomnia more than imagination alters taste, the same way brain seizures make you smell things that are only in your head. Perhaps the time has come to apply poultices to her forehead. She laughs and drinks a sip of glacier water, from the Stanley, while Jacques, despite claiming to be bushed, climbs the kitchen wall and, motionless, facing an overhang near the ceiling, assumes his monkey hang.

They are thinking the same thing and both laugh at the same time, acknowledging the outrageousness of their chosen practices.

▲ Insomnia has followed Maddie to the rat-free land of triumphant water. Jacques is out climbing frozen waterfalls in the Ghost. A region, he told her, difficult to access and where roads, such as they are, and bridges are often washed out and where vehicles get bogged down in streams, mud, snowbanks.

She does not understand the subtleties of his passion. Does not know what's what in the climbing world, but, since the squabble over glacier water, she refuses to interfere, only grateful that he continues to bring her water from les hauteurs, only happy that he is un bon gars who indulges her onion practice, even though he doesn't know what's what in the *Allium* world.

Nuit blanche after nuit blanche, she dreams experiments awake.

Batik pearls. Maddie twists thin blue rubber bands in a random pattern around each peeled pearl. Steeps the onions in salted beet juice. Goes to work on an overcast, freezing March day, dressing department store windows in frilly Easter garb. Goes back home to catch a few hours of sleep in Jacques's deserted bed. After two days of leaving them to steep in their glass vessel, she checks on her onions. Removes the thin elastic bands to reveal tiny white veins snaking around the rose pearls.

Jacques at work, redoing a roof while a chinook wind blows. Maddie after work, making amber pearls. She steeps a fresh batch of the vegetables in an infusion of saffron and the skins of Bermuda onion, which impart the rich colour of fossilized resin.

Jacques at home, climbing his gym walls, viewing Maddie's creations exhibited in glass bowls: I'm impressed, ma grande.

More. I want more. Perle noire, Jacques. The ultimate chic cocktail onion.

Another sleepless night. Jacques sleeping, Maddie searching. How do I get black pearls, Mom?

Lillian takes her time sending this postcard:

Perle noire, Madeleine? It reminds me of the black pearl of the Chinese empress dowager, placed in her mouth immediately after her death. Black lacquers? Deadly. Crushed kalonji seeds? Would the black of the wild onion seeds leach into the solution? How about squid ink? You are the empirical one, Madeleine. I can only theorize.

▲ Jacques is out climbing again. Will be gone for days. Went to a region called the Bugaboos, a place, he told her, of rock spires and hanging glaciers. Maddie goes back to basics. Amber, coral, black are mere distractions. Since she has been using her glacier water, she has often observed that the salt solution in which her pure white pearls steep is cloudy. She has refused to admit it, and yet, the evidence is clear.

Mom, help me. What should I do? I'm at my wits' end.

Lillian sends this postcard:

My poor Madeleine, no wonder. Your glacier water is no good for pickling. Before sending you to Calgary, I should have anticipated the problem of hard water. But then, you would not have met Jacques. Is he careful? Soft water is best for pickles.

Maddie's vision blurs. How could Mom be so wrong? Maddie knows, empirically speaking, that glacier water makes a tastier pearl. She has even reconciled herself with the water from the Athabasca. Recognized her imagination had tricked her. Jacques is a roofer, Mom. He lives on the high ground. Ancient water. Maddie knows she is right.

Her vision clears. She reads on:

However, if the mineral salts are in solution, you may have to distill the water. Will you go so far as to acquire a still or a retort? I feel for your difficulties in your Allium *world. I'm reading* Ulysses *and I'm turning insomniac too. An uphill struggle that your gentle bookish climber may know well. Oh, les montagnes et les Irlandais!*

A day later, Lillian sends this postcard via Priority Post:

I don't want to interfere with your onions or your personal life, but I just read that a young Québécois was killed in the mountains last week. The ancient Greeks believed garlic strengthened warriors before a battle and athletes before a contest.

Jacques comes back from his mountains, as always, bringing her a few litres of precious water. But he returns from the Bugaboos with no voice. During his multi-pitch climbs, his vocal cords suffered tiny tears from shouting in the cold against a howling wind.

Silently, he forms the words: Communication is paramount, ma grande.

When he had a booming voice, he did tell her that clear communication between two partners during a climb was more important than good communication in a relationship, unless, he went on with his head cocked to one side, a grin on his face, unless the couple in question also climbed together. In climbing, elliptic talk could be fatal.

Fatal? She asked him to explain further.

You're the lead climber. So, off you go making your way up a route while your partner belays you from below. Along the way, you put in pieces of protection, so if you fall, the last piece of protection will hold you—if it is placed properly—but only if your partner has you on a firm belay. All's going well. You get to the top and have not yet secured yourself, but, for some reason, your partner thinks you yelled secure and he takes you off belay. The rope becomes academic and the final word of the day is splat. Clear communication, ma grande. So, wind or no wind, you yell your little lungs out.

Yes, she could see that. On this night of Jacques being voiceless, an ancient lore lurks in the back of her mind. She spots the right postcard high up near the ceiling and she eyes the leeks languishing in the window boxes. She knows what she must do.

Wait. I'll be right back.

She rushes to the supermarket. Brings home, not the bacon, but leeks. Before he left, she had failed to give Jacques garlic. She will never forget again. From now on, he will eat garlic galore. Otherwise, what? This time, his vocal cords tearing? Next time, the climbing rope tearing? And then, and then. She can't bear the word "splat." And so, tonight, she will fortify him and will give him back his voice.

No spoon, Jacques. Hold the bowl with both hands, like for the tea ceremony. Drink slowly. Do you like it?

He articulates silently: Best vichyssoise I ever tasted.

It's not vichyssoise. No potato in it. Pure leeks and cream and water. Water from the Saskatchewan Glacier. Potage glacé du glacier. Does it help?

Jacques is not saying. Rather, he melts. Gestures for more potage aux poireaux. Swirls the tender green cream laced with the mild onion juice against his damaged vocal cords. Breathes in the bouquet to augment the wonderful palate expanding in his mouth. Feels the swell of scented smoothness sliding down his throat, silk and velvet both, soothing. He licks his bowl, he licks his chops, his eyes become languid, his hand softens on hers. Oh, he is beyond mere desire.

You see, Jacques, the power of your glacier water. Despite containing mineral salts. Your mouth is the living proof that the water gave my leek brew its character. I suppose Mom is wrong. The mineral salts don't harm my pearls. I must be imagining things again. Now, practise your calls. Be clear, if not loud.

Secure. Off belay. The words grate against the still irritated vocal cords: On belay. Climbing. Tension. Great soup.

Bah! it's all folklore, Jacques.

He looks for one of Lillian's narratives. Finds it pinned high above the western window. He climbs up and reads in a husky voice:

*The ancient Egyptians, Romans and Celts were great admirers of the leek (*Allium porrum*). The Roman satirist Juvenal wrote that "Egypt is a country where onions are adored and leeks are gods." The Romans, not to be outdone in the leek mystique, believed the hardy, biennial herbaceous cousin of your beloved pearl was beneficial for the vocal cords. Nero, ma chérie, drank leek soup to clarify and deepen his voice for speechmaking. I am left to wonder if French chef Louis Diat's American creation, vichyssoise, ever had or still has as far-reaching political ramifications in Washington, DC. Has the leek ever set the town on fire?*

As he downclimbs, Jacques rattles on his vital calls in a shaky singsong: On belay. Secure. Climbing. Once safe on the ground, he pins the postcard closer to his climbing gear.

They fall into bed. Jacques loving Maddie. Maddie loving Jacques. He moves with a grace that always surprises her. Around her curves or on his climbing walls, he is all feathery grace. Grace despite a short, stout body with thighs the size of cedar posts. His blood belongs to the sturdy race of coureurs des bois. His ancestors may very well have survived on a diet of wild chicagou, as père Marquette had on the south shore of lac Michigan. Jacques Lachance with his roof-tar hair and raven eyes will always come back from his mountains with glacier water and tales of glory. On Mondays, after his weekend climbs, he will always be up on someone's roof laying asphalt shingles and nailing them down with his big nail gun.

She will not sleep and she will make the perfect pickled onion yet.

▲ Early this morning, Maddie went to market and bought a twenty-pound sack of pearls from her Hutterite man. He winked at her, the sweet man in black, the country man staring at the women in the city. His face smooth as mother-of-pearl under his rough oyster-shell clothing. She paid and winked back.

Back home, she blanches batch after batch of pearls to loosen the skin. Considers the tedium of the work ahead, and the day so hot.

Standing at the counter, Maddie skins, glancing at a postcard propped against the backsplash:

Ah, the French with their idées reçues! Hear Anatole France
babble: "Les poireaux sont les asperges du pauvre." Didn't he
know about the Welsh? In 640, ma chérie, they wore leeks on

their caps and triumphed over the Saxons. I hate to imagine
what their fate would have been if they had worn asparagus.

Maddie is skinning onions and Jacques is climbing hard rock
in a canyon where, he told her, Indian petroglyphs of hunters on
white waters are still visible on the rock walls. She should have
fixed a leek to his climbing helmet. She wonders if, last night,
she didn't go overboard with the onion feast she served in bed.

They began with Gibsons. She judged her cocktail pearls not
perfect. Not yet.

Forget the pearls, Madeleine. Get tipsy. You need a good
night's sleep. You need a thousand good nights' sleep.

While sipping gin and vermouth, they nibbled on tiny onion
sandwiches made with slices of brioche and rolled in chopped
parsley.

Parsley, good for the breath, ma grande. I'm fed up with
roofers' jokes about onion breath.

Jacques is away climbing. Maddie is peeling, the silvery skins
clinging to her fingers. She concentrates on her onion repast.

Then, she brought flamiche, a leek pie, which she garnished
with roasted cloves of garlic. Jacques's eyes shone less bright.

Then, she served onion soup à la Casey, the beef stock
for which, she told him, had to simmer eight hours a day for
three days, before the final simmering with a quantity of thinly
sliced...

Onions. Tomorrow, I'm climbing a rock route that is 5.13.

Is that difficult?

I've never climbed above 5.12. To give you an idea of 5.12,
think of circus acrobats or contortionists. To give you an idea of
5.13, think of Spider-Man without his spider silk. 5.13 is pretty
close to the edge of defying gravity.

Does the soup taste a little bitter to you?

I'm excited, but nervous. This might end in bitter
disappointment. He grinned rather grimly. Sipped his soup.

La pièce de résistance was caramelized shallots with
brochettes of lamb. Jacques's spirit rose as he sank his teeth into
the red meat.

Tomorrow while you climb, I'll go to market. With so many
onions, I'll be able to sort them precisely by size. I'll measure
the diameter of each pearl. That way, when they're ready to
be cooked, I'll be able to calculate more accurately how many
seconds each batch must stay in the boiling water.

Jacques bared his teeth at her.

She smiled a tight little smile: I'm entering my 5.13 phase,
Jacko baby. Measuring the diameter of pearls before cooking
them is pretty extreme.

They rinsed their mutual apprehension and palates with a red
onion and orange salad, heavily laced with Italian parsley.

For your breath, Jacques. So tomorrow, while belaying you,
your climbing partner will spare you disparaging remarks. And
will resist the temptation to drop you. Splat. I will not hear of it.

He narrowed his eyes: And for dessert, Madeleine? Garlic ice
cream?

Don't laugh.

Who's laughing?

They do it in California.

Figures. I'll make black coffee. You, have more Gibsons.
Tonight, I want you to knock yourself out.

If Maddie slept, it was in a fitful gin-induced stupor. And
heard him sneak out of the house at dawn, knowing he didn't
have to leave that early. Is Maddie hanging herself with her rope
of onions while Jacques climbs? While Jacques is exhibiting
signs of onion fatigue? Or, last night, was he truly experiencing
the jitters about today's climb? She rinses the onion skins off her

hands and goes for a run, leaving the naked pearls strewn about the kitchen counter. Damn it, she's gonna sleep a real sleep tonight.

▲ Maddie's nuits blanches in Bowness are getting colder. Even in August. Jacques sleeps with reckless abandon in the monkey hang position, as if his bed were the smooth, overhanging monolith of his last climb and his pillow the bulge, he told her, the crux he failed to climb over. No matter how often he tried and tried and tried, he kept falling and falling and falling. While Jacques dreams of climbing success above his level of competence, Maddie shivers. She touches the small of his back, her cold hand on his warm skin. Jacques doesn't so much as stir. For lack of dreaming, Maddie's brain hanging on the edge of the precipice of wakefulness will invent hallucinations. No longer will the warmth of Jacques Lachance's strong-agile body abandoned to the night save her from plunging to the ground of terminal exhaustion.

She gets up. Not long after her arrival, they partitioned sleep and insomnia. She insisted. She could not bear robbing him of his dreams. So, he built a wall to enclose the bed. When Maddie roams, chops, pickles, she imprisons Jacques in the cubbyhole of his bed. He made the partition with hinges to flatten it when not in use, so as not to impede his wall-climbing practice. Now, he sleeps, she roams the night. And shivers.

She crushes yellow onions, all the onions she can find in the house. Skin and all, she crushes *cepa*, her chef's knife dripping with *Allium* juice, her face wet with onion tears. She weighs skin, flesh and juice on her kitchen scale, then transfers everything to her stockpot. Fills the pot with a mixture of glacier water, all the samples left in the house. Brings the mash to a boil and lets the brew simmer until the water turns a deep amber.

She reads the postcard by the south window where the herbaceous chives and scallions and leeks now thrive in their boxes:

Every winter, ma chérie, your paternal grandmother made onion-water. Contre les rhumes et la grippe, your papa told me. The antibiotic properties of the cepa were powerless against cold and flu viruses. But your grandmother called everything microbes, whether bacteria, viruses, fungi or germs. Anything smaller than a fruit fly was a microbe. And microbes make you sick. And microbes never survive the smell and taste of onions. To your grandmother, this was a fact, simply because it came to her from her deep ancestral past. True up to a point, onion-water had its benefits, as diuretic, expectorant, mild heart booster. It gave the family heart. Ça nous donnait du coeur au ventre, your grandma repeated. Your papa's family sailed onion-water all winter and landed safely on the healthy shores of spring. And there, they pulled out of the earth the newly sprung spring onions. And like pallid aphids, they sucked on the succulent green juice.

Maddie strains the spent flesh and skins of the resilient onions. Looks for sugar. They are out of cane sugar. Then notices the jar of Alberta unfiltered honey. She spoons two hundred grams of the bee's ambrosia into her onion-water and boils down the liquid to a light syrup. She pours a small glass. Blows. Sniffs the scented vapours. Breath of bees. An ambrosial brew made of thousands of compounds mixed in minute quantity through the action of earth, sun, water, and in the workshop of the winged honey makers. Maddie dips the tip of her tongue into the elixir. Takes a sip. Swirls and breathes in. Success! At long last, she may have come to the end of her search. With urgency, she notes her findings in her lab book.

She has landed in the sweet land of triumphant water and ambrosial honey. She checks the label, the beekeeper's address right there, black on pale yellow. Now, there's a man sure of his practice. She checks the map of Alberta. She has found her centre, her western centre, between Jacques Lachance's glaciated water in the high mountains to the west, her Hutterite sweet pearl grower in the south and now, her sugar maker on the northern prairies loving his bees, tending them tender so they may make their perfect alfalfa-clover honey. Honey that will transform even the poorest vinegar into the perfect pickles. She must go lightly on the vinegar. At last, she has climbed the crux of her search. Victory close at hand exploding her white nights. Searching, watchful restlessness, finding. In Jacques Lachance's Bowness bungalow, in the centre of her equilateral triangle, she dances, onion-fashion, in concentric circles.

She opens all the windows to air the house. Unhinges the bed partition. Snuggles up against Jacques's warm flank. Sweet love, Jacques, quelle chance. She sleeps.

▲ September. Maddie sends Lillian a postcard:

Mom, the September light here is magnificent.

In the September light, while Jacques climbs something not so gravity-defying, Maddie chops vast quantities of onions. Steel blade against bulb, she slices through membrane. The sulphurous vapour hypnotizes her into the stillness of the moment. Through onion eyes, she sees quivering shapes. Pictures herself walking knee-deep into fields of the white shallots of Megara. The setting sun painting the stone walls of the ancient city onion-ochre. Through onion tears, she sees Jacques clinging to rock. Imagines the blue water of glaciers. And superimposed on the limestone walls of the Rockies, she sees the shadows of cotton-wrapped pyramid builders biting into onions, their daily bread, before lifting huge stones that they stack into monuments of foolishness.

In the September light, Jacques climbs closer to his desire. In two litres of glacier water, Maddie boils down two kilos of white onions to their essence. Strains the mother liquor for her thousand-year-old pearls. Pours one hundred and twenty grams of Alberta honey into the one and one-half litres of onion-flavoured elixir. Adds a mere hint of good white wine vinegar from France (after all, her distant ancestors on Papa's side should be a factor in this difficult chemical reaction).

Maddie boils two hundred grams of same-size, skinned, salt-steeped pearls exactly seventy-two seconds. Packs them in sterilized glass jars. Pours the hot pickling juice over them. Holds the spices. The result must be pure, naked *cepa*. She seals the jars and allows the pearls to mature for one month in a cool dark place. As Mom wrote about the thousand-year egg, "some period of burial must be accepted."

One month later, Maddie carefully wraps a small jar of perfect pickled pearls and sends it to the other end of the continent.

The September light has shifted to the darkening short days of autumn. Maddie props on the table Lillian's latest postcard:

That translator Jowett wrote: "They will have a relish—salt, and olives, and cheese, and onions." I too will treat myself. Thank you for the jar of thousand-year-old pearls. They are truly delectable. As you had wished. To honour your achievement, ma chérie, I will unlock the kitchen and feast on freshly baked crusty bread, firm sweet butter and five-year-old cheddar. I believe, the perfect accompaniment to your perfect pearls. And I will toast you and your climber with a silver mug of best

stout. You've reached the end of your search. Are you happy?
Will you sleep?

▲ Jacques and Maddie sit at the table under the western window.
They nibble on Maddie's pickled ambrosial pearls.

I have to admit, ma grande, I never thought a pickled onion
could be so. So...

Not too pungent?

Pungent? He pops another pearl into his mouth. Bites. Eyes
half-closed, his taste buds in a state of ecstasy, he chews slowly.
Swallows. Superb, he says, his voice dreamy. Simply superb. This,
my alchemist Zoé Madeleine Rivière, redefines pungent.

. Truly? You feel it too? A true taste desire?

He grins, his head cocked to one side: You've climbed the
crux of the matter. And he reads her lab book. You have a winner
here. You should publish this.

Ha! At last, I pickled my perfect thousand-year-old pearl.
That's good enough for me.

She gets up from the table, grabs various holds on the
climbing walls: By the way, Jack Lastchance. Never thought of
asking. Do you keep a journal of your climbs?

He looks up from her lab book: Sure, I do. And he touches his
temples. Here. Every single feature of a climb recorded. And he
touches his heart and thigh muscles and lungs. And here and
here and here. Every move.

She shakes her head. Hauls herself off the floor a tad. Doesn't
dare go higher. A tad is a beginning. Turns toward Jacques: What
do you climbers do after Everest and K2? After all the big walls
have been climbed? What do you do for an encore?

It very much depends on the climber.

Maddie paces up and down between the southern and
western windows, eyeing the planters. Then, she starts to pull

the mature leeks and scallions and chives out of the soil.

What are you doing?

Thrips. Mom says aphids avoid garlic. But thrips thrive on onions.

How did they get into the house?

I'm getting rid of everything.

Everything? Sounds final. Jacques's face freezes. You're not thinking of relocating, are you?

Maddie shivers with disgust as she squashes the little pests by the dozen. She swears she hears their screams at the approaching giant fingers. Their screams of agony as she squishes them. Then, she itches all over: I'm really, really tired of onions.

Oh.

Oh, what, Jacques?

I had a surprise for you. That's oh.

Une surprise? Tell me.

Better show you.

He grabs her by the arm and brings her into the narrow yard. And there stands the sculpture of a gigantic dazzling-white head of garlic.

Jacques grins at Maddie's puzzled face: I made it with chicken wire and plaster. You like it? Do you like it?

Like it! It's fantastic. What will you do with it?

I'll put it on the roof.

An onion-cum-garlic dome?

Sure. For our onion house. I started making a big onion. But don't you think a garlic head is more interesting? You'll help me hoist it up on the roof. I'll rope it and we'll lift it and attach it up there.

Do you have a ladder?

Ladder? We're going to do a bit of climbing, you and I.

You may know your onions climbing. I...

High time you learned. And after this little practice, you'll come with me to see, and feel, where your glacier water came from.

I'm through with onion cookery.

You'll be perfectly safe.

Climbing the Bowness bungalow with the high slanting roof does seem a ridiculous idea, but Jacques has been so patient, putting up with months of onion and vinegar fumes, and now wanting to show his love for her to the entire neighbourhood by installing the head of garlic on his roof, Jacques, so sweet, la soigne aux petits oignons, treating her like a queen, how can she refuse. Maddie chokes a little.

Truly, Jacques. What do you do after you've climbed all the big mountains?

He laughs as he wraps the sculpture in a large net, which he ties to a nylon cord before securing the other end of the cord to his harness.

What do we do, ma grande? We start all over.

She puts on an old pair of Jacques's rock shoes. They're so tight, she feels like the Chinese empress dowager's daughter. He slips a harness on her and ties one end of the climbing rope through it with a figure-eight rewoven knot. Then he drags the other end of the rope tied behind his harness and, in two steps, it seems to Maddie, he is up on the roof. He describes what he is doing, as if she had a clue. He rigs a belay station around the base of the chimney and will belay Maddie from up there.

When the rope is taut at her harness, he tells her she is ready to climb: On belay! His voice is leeky, loud and clear.

She doesn't move.

Don't worry. I got you in case you fall.

In case? You've got to be joking. She laughs softly. Stares at the smooth wall. Wonders how on earth he did it. Giggling, she yells, in a not-too-convinced voice: Climbing.

Climb on! His voice is full of conviction for the two of them.

Yes, but. How? She tries and slips even before leaving the yard. Looks and looks at the wood siding. This is impossible. How does he do it? He must have secret suction cups all over him. At last, she notices tiny ledges between the planks and other nodules of imperfection in the siding for her fingers to grab and for her big toes to rest on. With a mixture of terror and exhilaration, she manages to haul herself off the ground. After her tenth fall, each complete with a sharp, short scream and her heart climbing into her throat at the speed of an excited rat scaling inner walls, she lets her body discover its own balance.

She actually climbs. In a perverted mix of fear and pleasure, she actually *enjoys* this vertical walking. Pungent desire.

Now. She faces the crux. How do you climb over the eaves? She wishes Jacques had given her a bit of advance warning, so she could have prepared by eating a whole head of garlic to give herself the Greek courage of warriors and the endurance of athletes. Overhang, how do you overcome the overhang? She has seen him do the move often enough on his climbing walls. But watching and doing are not the same. The gulf separating the theoretical and the empirical.

She tries the monkey hang, but her arms are dying on her, her calves shake, the whole house shakes with her shaking. And she falls, and falls, dangling in mid-air, held by the rope. She growls in frustration, in jealousy of Jacques's ease and, finally, in anger. Anger gives her the impetus to hold on to the edge of the roof, as sticky and slippery as decaying onions. A couple more moves, scraping her knees on the aluminum trough, grating her hands on the rough shingles, and she crawls on all fours. Stands up on the roof. Jacques pulls in slack and she walks uphill toward him, holding on to the rope with both hands, quite aware of the force of gravity on the sharp angle of that terrain. He clips her in to the belay station.

He shouts playfully: Secure! Normally, you're responsible for clipping in yourself. And you're the one who has to say secure, loud and clear, before your partner can take you off belay. He kisses her. Wasn't this fun?

A whole hour it took me!

Don't exaggerate.

How embarrassing. I'll eat onion-stuffed crow for a week, Jacques. How dare you rat on me to your climbing buddies. So embarrassing.

You made it, Maddie. First try. You climbed the Bowness Bungalow route.

They both laugh, hoisting the head of garlic. Jacques fastens it to the apex of the roof. It gleams in the autumn sun.

For the first time, Maddie realizes how high above the street they stand: How will we get down?

Rappel. I'll teach you rappelling. You'll love it.

Love it? She's not so sure, but she must believe. What's the alternative? Live on the roof with the big garlic?

Maddie can almost touch the snow-capped rocks rising against the perfect blue western sky. She fancies she can hear glacier water running. She looks at Jacques. He squints at her.

L'air des montagnes, Maddie. Wait until you breathe that mountain air. After one day up there, you will sleep like never before. I promise. Best sleep in the world.

You've always known your onions, Jacques.

He breaks into that grin of his.

They gaze at the grey limestone walls leaning against the distance. Jacques, full of promise and expectation. They gaze at the giant head of garlic tied to the chimney. One day, perhaps, a strong chinook will send the sculpture crashing down along the property line. Maddie studies Jacques's face, wondering how she got herself from her warped Montréal apartment to this unreal land.

What's wrong with this picture, Jacques?

Wrong? He squints at the distance. Then looks at her: From where we stand, ma grande, not one single thing I can see.

He holds her in his strong arms, against his strong heart, gently blowing into her face his sweet perfect-pickled-pearl breath.

You and I, my onion lady, are just fine.

Nepal / High

THE PEOPLE of Borlang Bhanjyang are positive.
The yeti killed Jeanne. He took her in the middle
of the night. Dragged her out of the mud house and
carried her into the heart of the Himalayas. Didn't
they find her broken body at the foot of a cliff?
The woman where Jeanne is staying, the mother of
Jeanne's mountain guide, Rana, can't stop herself
from beating her breast and wailing, imploring
the Nepalese gods and goddesses to forgive her
negligence. The wooden panel closing the window.
Left open. On the shadowy night.

The inhabitants of this hamlet of five houses
perched on a hill between three deep valleys are
gathered together in front of the low door. They tell a
long story Rachel does not understand. Except the
word yeti that they repeat over and over.

They show Rachel the famous window through
which the creature entered the room. The poor beast
couldn't be much bigger than a cat to have managed
to slide through such a small opening. Jeanne and
the yeti, a new legend taking form. A story to be told
from village to village, the tale that will expand over
long winter evenings. Jeanne who could not stand still.

Rana asks Rachel what she wants to do with the body. She looks at him, not understanding. She is dreaming. When she wakes up, Jeanne will be there, as skinny as ever, as ready as ever to mock Rachel's concerns. The body? What body, Rana?

Two men enter the low-ceilinged room, carrying a stretcher covered with layers of colourful light fabrics topped with wildflowers. They set down their burden on the beaten-earth floor and exit without a word. Even though the villagers have returned to their own concerns and gone home for their evening meal and even though only Rana, his mother and his maybe seven-year-old brother remain in the room already darkened by night, Rachel feels dozens of eyes watching her next move.

She stares at the fabrics, notes the freshness of the yellow flowers. Doesn't dare lift the diaphanous shroud. What does a mutilated corpse look like? Maybe Jeanne sustained fatal injuries to her internal organs, leaving her body intact on the outside. Rachel can't bring herself to look.

She gingerly feels the shape lying under silk. A vaporous coldness enters her fingertips to freeze her to the elbow. It is rigid, that thing she touched, the arm of her dead cousin. What was she doing outside in the middle of the night? Restless Jeanne. See how still you are now.

Rana? Can we have her cremated? Can we burn her on a funeral pyre, according to your customs?

Rana nods: Yes. Jeanne, she was my sister.

Something else. Her things. She brought things with her to Borlang Bhanjyang. Photos, recordings, from her previous stop. When she went to Tibet.

Rana's eyes brighten and he shows her a metal box in the small space reserved for the dead woman. He then joins his mother and brother, both silent at the other end of the room where a tiny fire burns.

The Nepalese night tightens its grip around the hamlet, over the big mountains, while the wind carries the story of the Western woman who came to join her mother in death, the story whispered all the way to the highest summits where her spirit will be preserved in the thin air of eternal cold. They all came here to die. Jeanne's mother. Rachel's father. And now, Jeanne herself. End game.

Stooping on account of the low ceiling, Rachel moves closer to the group gathered around the fire. Without that small flame burning in the hearth dug in the floor, it would be pitch-dark. From time to time, Rachel glances behind her. Through the flickering flame, it seems to her that something is moving under those layers of cloth.

All at once, in this house at the far reaches of the world, the deep fatigue and stress accumulated over this long, long day pull her down into the earthen floor. Only this morning on the streets of Kathmandu, she never doubted she was on her way to meet Jeanne. Alive.

An accident? What accident?

▲ Rana found Rachel in the small hotel on the outskirts of Kathmandu where Jeanne had asked her to wait for her. And waiting, that's what Rachel had been doing. For days. Hiking the Himalayas around Kathmandu. Perhaps as far as the Helambu region, from where many a mountain guide hails. That had been the plan. Simple. But with Jeanne, the simplest thing always became convoluted. True. Afterward, the game was worth the candle. So, Rachel waited. This morning before dawn, the innkeeper rapped on her door. A man was asking for Miss Rachel. He was waiting in the dining room.

The man introduced himself as Rana. Jeanne had hired him to guide them on a few treks, perhaps in the Helambu, perhaps...

Yes, yes, Rachel knew the plan. Why...

Perhaps even as far as Base Camp at Sagarmāthā and...

Sagarmāthā?

Chomolungma. The many names of Mount Everest.

Yes, yes, Rachel knew that too, but. Chomo was not in the plan. Half-asleep, she feared she was missing important facts. Did Jeanne change their plan and now wanted to trek *all the way* to Base Camp? Rachel wasn't in top shape for that kind of trekking.

Miss Rachel's shape did not matter.

Maybe not to him, but it sure did to her. Why was her daffy cousin waiting outside and sending the guide to do the talking for her?

Jeanne was in his native village of Borlang Bhanjyang...

Where was Bor-jyang?

In the mountains. A few hours' walk from here.

What was she doing in the mountains? They were supposed to go in the mountains together. Why the change of plan? This was maddening.

So, too, was it for Rana, apparently, who tried to stay focused.

So, what was Rachel supposed to do?

Miss Rachel had to come right away.

Right this minute? It was still night.

Please, Miss Rachel.

Okay okay, would the guide give her a minute? She must get her pack, gather her things, gather her thoughts, forget nothing. She hurried back upstairs. Damn damn damn Jeanne! Rachel hated rushed departure.

When she came back down, fully loaded and in a foul mood, Rana held the door for her. She felt bad. Why take it out on him? She relaxed her face and that's when he told her.

There was an accident.

An accident? What accident?

Woodsmoke in her eyes. Woodsmoke in her lungs. Words spoken low in a tongue Rachel does not understand. Darkness compressing against bones. Behind her back, Jeanne. Dead. Jeanne's mother and Rachel's father, sister and brother in love with the world and who died in the world, somewhere not far from here. The cousins' growing years, punctuated by the unimaginable parental vanishing act. The act connecting the two girls beyond blood alone. The endless speculations. The fairy tale returns. The heroic rescue missions they would mount. And then, the call of the mountains. The same lure that took Jeanne's mother, that captured Rachel's father. The girls learned mountaineering, so that one day, they would find, what? A long time ago, Rachel stopped believing the unbelievable. Not so Jeanne. Oh, yes. She knew her mother was beyond rescue. But whereas the endless game of questions and answers no longer mattered to Rachel, Jeanne had never given up the need to know what how why. And where. So, here they came, under the pretence of a trekking trip, to discover at last some kind of an answer. And tonight, so close and forever too far, nothing will get resolved. Rachel, alone somewhere in the world, alone with her memories and her burns. Alone with the burden of a very old fatigue. And no one with whom to share any of it. No one. There was only Jeanne. Rachel closes her teary eyes and holds her fitful breath against that woodsmoke.

▲ In Kathmandu this morning, after thunderstorms and torrential rain, the sky was clear and the cleansed air smelling of wet earth. The sun was still low between the quiet houses, but the light presaged a fresh beginning.

Rana guides Rachel to Sundarijal, a village on the other side of the valley where they will reach the trailhead and climb into

the Kathmandu foothills. For now, a road crosses rice fields
through which a soft wind runs, bending the young green shoots
of the second planting.

In the countryside, daily activities have begun. The regular
sound of a water pump. Hand threshing. From wide bamboo
sieves, women throw grains into the air, the straw falling back on
them in a gold rain. On the ground, red chilies drying in the sun
fill the air with their sweet scent and their sharp capsicum sting.

Compared to Rana, used to tramp up and down his vertical
land, Rachel walks slowly, only beginning to reacquaint herself
with her mountaineer's legs, the practice abandoned for all
the wrong reasons. Work, daily life, but mainly because Jeanne
had been away too long and Rachel was not very good at
prompting herself, she explains to the guide who shows no sign
of impatience. He slows down his pace, waits for her, is vague
when, a little out of breath, she asks him about the accident.
How serious could it be? With Jeanne, one never knows what to
expect. As if there were no urgency, and perhaps there is none,
they stop for chai at the local stall. They unload themselves of
their burden, Rachel her backpack, Rana a huge basket that he
carries on his back held by a strap slung across his forehead.

Rana sips the spiced tea and talks softly: Family, it is the
link with the earth. It is the natal land, something above one's
own life. We can rely on family, lean on family. In our houses
in the evenings when the family gathers around the fire, it is
the sweetest moment of the day. But families are beginning
to fall apart. Even here in Nepal where the tie has always been
strong. Young people like myself leave to see the world, to live
their own lives. Friends become more important. Even when the
friendships don't last. Family though. Even when it is far away,
family remains the tie that stretches beyond mountains. Beyond
cities, beyond ambitions. On the other hand, we don't choose

our family. If we come from a bad family, we can't disavow it, we can't cut the tie completely. Friends, we can choose. For good or for bad, friendship gives you more control. Let's go. It's getting late.

After the spill of words, Rana keeps quiet, except for the business of the trek. And the climb begins.

In sections of the trail, Rachel slips in thick mud, in others, she twists her ankles on the rocky ground, the soil washed away during weeks of monsoon. The elevation gain is gradual, and relentless. A vice squeezes her lungs and she must stop often, bending over in an attempt to loosen up her diaphragm. Rana waits for her to catch her breath.

The trail climbs up, Rachel's thigh muscles tense up, her mind runs away from her, eager to assess the distance still to cover, her eyes fix the tip of her boots, her mouth counts steps. Eventually, like all highs, this slope will level off.

After three hours, the trekker and her guide reach a small plateau supporting two houses. Terraced paddy fields surround the modest dwellings.

Borlang Bhanjyang?

Rana shakes his head, pointing at infinity, not interrupting his walk uphill.

Rachel's blood is boiling, swelling the veins on her hands, making sausages of her fingers. She is dripping with sweat. As soon as a hill rises to hide the sun, she shivers in the humid air. To catch up to Rana, she takes off her boots and cuts across the paddy fields. The lukewarm water cools her down. She is dreaming of a slow swim in one of the lakes in the Laurentians of home. She and Jeanne. Kids on holiday, splashing each other under the gentle but watchful eye of Rachel's widowed mother. Then she sees her guide crouching on a rock, his knees in his armpits, gesticulating and laughing.

She takes heart from his bonhomie, only to notice, back on dry ground, that her feet are covered with leeches. Rana removes the annelids and she wipes her bloody feet. As she laces her boots, the sun sets below the jagged horizon. Although the sky is still full of light, dusk darkens the forest. They must hurry.

To Rachel's relief, the trail goes down toward a valley. Soon, in a forest of rhododendrons, the ground becomes steep again. How did Jeanne react to this land? Knowing her cousin, the bigger the challenge the louder she'd trumpet her enjoyment. Make yourself tough, Rach. That, Jeanne's mantra to Rachel from their childhood on. Did tough Jeanne break a leg, too much in a hurry? Here, what was her rush? Ahead, Rana is still walking simply, steadily, as if on flat ground, not even bothered by the basket heavy with supplies that he has been carrying since departure this morning.

As soon as the trail levels off again, Rachel removes her pack and sits on a rock, trying to control her breathing and the shaking in her calf muscles. Evening is fast falling and Borlang lies at the edge of the world. She resumes the trek, emptying her mind of all thoughts, fixing her eyes on nothing.

In the sky, the greying of daylight deepens. With many gestures, Rana encourages his client to keep moving. They are almost there.

How long?

Only one hour.

One hour!

Low clouds have entered the forest. Despite the altitude, the jungle damp is oppressive. Between patches of fog, rotting fallen trees are covered with thick moss hanging off the logs.

At this hour between dog and wolf, between tiger and yeti, in this land between sky and equator, with utter exhaustion in her muscles and dangerous impatience in her heart, the phantasmagoria unfolding could easily throw Rachel over the edge. She touches the old scar across her forehead, the thin white line, testimony to childhood games, invariably of Jeanne's invention.

Tripping over her boots, she walks to ward off small fears. The closer she gets to be reunited with her cousin, the more she convinces herself it was a mistake to have accepted her invitation. The slope is so steep, she smells the earth, the acrid wet soil teeming with countless bacteria decomposing. Everything.

The more she walks, the longer the trail. Her clothes are soaked through and she can't stop shivering. In the darkness now engulfing the forest, she loses the trail just as the ground becomes horizontal. She emerges on another treeless plateau, Rana out of sight. From this clearing, she watches the horizon reddened by the setting sun, the bank of clouds hiding the big peaks, though she senses their imposing presence. She can almost taste the faraway snow. Rana calls her from the other side of the trees. She runs to join him.

In the dark, the trail manifests itself again. Rachel re-enters the forest. Soon, she reaches a rise. Borlang. Five low-slung houses made of mud bricks and stone line both sides of the trail, the trail that goes on to the next hamlet. Borlang Bhanjyang, civilization, the refuge against night terrors. The place where Rachel will be reunited with Jeanne.

Water is boiling over the tiny fire. A lit cigarette between her lips, eyes half-closed against the smoke, the woman throws loose tea leaves into a dented pot. Pours boiling water over the leaves. Gives Rachel a glass of sweetened tea. The scalding brew brings on a sigh of pleasure to the trekker depleted of energy.

The tea erases fatigue, not her loss. The sugar relaxes her smashed muscles, not the stiff stillness of her cousin. She

forgets the muddy trail washed away by monsoon rains, the
bloodsuckers latched on to her feet, not Jeanne's broken body
already decomposing under the fresh wildflowers. She sips her
tea and suppresses a sob.

The woman prepares chapatis. Mixes flour and water. Kneads
the dough. Shapes a thin disk between her palms. Stokes up the
fire by blowing in the hollow of a length of bamboo. Cooks the
bread on an iron griddle. Chats in a low voice with Rana and her
younger son. Drops the flat bread in the embers until the dough
blisters.

Rachel slowly chews on the warm chapati. By the fire, familiar
gestures protect her from night and darkness surrounding the
house, from shapes undefined but alive. What were you looking
for out there, Jeanne?

Jeanne had called Rachel. Three notes played on a reed flute.
As always, Rachel answered the call. And here they are, both
cousins reunited in this place where hot embers are preciously
kept alive for everyone to share. A cluster of mud houses perched
at the edge of breathable air. Jeanne and Rachel no longer
playing the game of rescue, the game of being benighted in the
mountains where their parents disappeared. They are here at
last. In the middle of the Himalayas. A flute played, the scent of
flowers wafting from a cadaver, Jeanne no longer directing the
game. Jeanne's heavy presence latching on to Rachel's spine.

For the hundredth time, the Nepalese woman ensures the
window is securely latched. To keep the yeti from abducting
woman or child or the deceased and carrying them away.
Followed by the boy, the woman climbs the wooden stairs that
squeak in the dark. Rana rests his hand on Rachel's shoulder,
bidding her goodnight before disappearing behind his little
brother.

Woodsmoke. The mud house is full of smoke, smoke that
sticks to the skin, to the hair, smoke that stings the eyes, chokes

the lungs, smoke that embeds itself in clothing. And at dawn, Rachel will carry the smoke with her.

The yeti has not come back. The flute plays its funeral chant from mountain to mountain. Rachel lies down on the straw mat. Beside her, Jeanne sleeps.

I was always a little jealous of your daredevil ways, Jeanne. For a long time, I tried to emulate you, to catch the excitement you generated and make it my own. It never worked. I was not you. You remember at fourteen when you disappeared from our house? At last, I could breathe. Without you around to challenge me, I could go back to my habitual nonchalance. Over time, you came back, of course, but never to stay long. You caught me in your wake, and that was fun, because I knew it wouldn't last. And tonight, here we are. You called me back after more years of silence. And this time, you came out of your absence with your biggest daredevil scheme yet. And here I am to claim your body at the far end of the world, and in your death, Jeanne, you are more powerful than when you were alive.

I caught our parents' disease, Rachel. So consumed with exploration that I forgot to look in my own backyard. I so wanted to hold the world in one grasp, in its entirety, that anything nearby, anything inside me simply faded away. In the end, I saw nothing. I left my native soil and I'm far from the promised land. I left to chase an imaginary goose and I died alone, at the foot of a strange mountain, torn by my inner yeti. That is what you would like to believe, isn't it, Rach? True. I fenced you off inside a childhood in which I didn't let you speak. Jeanne the Great, queen of the game. In the end though, you're the one who must have been right since you are alive and I am not.

You, dead. I can't believe it. Maybe, you never existed, Jeanne. Always so full of extraordinary stories that only happened to you. While I never had anything much to tell other than my life, too dull to shine beside jeannesque adventures. When you disappeared from our house, I went to your bedroom daily. Such an empty room without you. It was glacial. I started doubting everything about you. After a few days, I became accustomed to your absence and I began to believe you had been nothing more than a figment of my imagination. My imaginary cousin, the enchanting one. Even your bed still bearing the imprint of your body on the sheet, of your head on the pillow was an illusion. And now, you reappear for the grand finale, resting on another kind of bed, calling me from deepest Asia. What story are you about to tell me?

In the dark, Rachel locates the metal trunk. In her backpack, she searches for a candle and lights it. The pale trembling halo causes the shape under the layers of fabric to appear gigantic. Rachel opens the trunk. Cans of films and audio recordings, snapshots, helter-skelter. Also, a portable tape recorder. She presses play. The batteries still have power.

The sound of a stream. Children playing, shouting. Jeanne's voice rises in the foreground, announcing that she is interviewing an old Tibetan man whose name escapes Rachel, from a village, the name of which Rachel doesn't quite catch.

Did you know Colette and Albert Boutin? They were sister and brother. Explorers.

I knew them well. They came here in 1962. I was a young man then. They hired me as their guide and interpreter. They came to film village life before the old ways disappeared. They are gone, but the old customs live on despite the occupation of our land by the Mandarins. The man chuckles. We are too remote even for the Chinese lords to reach us. I will give you the documents Colette and Albert made about us. It is only fair. You should have them. They may also bear witness to our past, should the Chinese decide to take an interest in us.

Where are the Boutins now? Where is Colette?

Oh, they died. A long, long time ago. You said she was your mother, Colette? She was a kind soul. I feel for you, Miss Jeanne.

How did she die?

She fell into a crevasse. When we found her, she was still alive. She died two days later. We did what we could. Too much cold had entered her heart. So very sorry.

And Albert? My mother's brother? Albert was my cousin's dad. She'll want to know.

Ah, yes, Albert. He was pretty high on chang, our local beer. We will have some later. It makes you gay and carefree. But Albert, he was so very sad. He told us, he drank to drown sadness. The more he drank, the sadder he became. He was broken by his sister's death. Your mother, you say? So very sorry. The next day, Albert said he needed to walk to sort himself out. He got lost in a snowstorm.

Where did you bury Colette?

Here, Miss Jeanne, we only bury two kinds of people. Those who died of a contagious disease and criminals.

So, you cremate the dead?

We do. But here in Tibet, cremation is reserved for learned monks and for persons of high rank. And water burial is for the very poor and beggars and widows and widowers.

Then, how did you... dispose of my mother's body?

We gave Colette the same funeral as for the majority of people. Her soul was properly released in a celestial burial.

What is that? A celestial burial?

We gave her body to the vultures.

Cut interview. Jeanne is doing a voice-over.

After my interview with the old guide, I shot and witnessed funerals similar to the one they gave my mother. A celestial burial. The rite of the vultures. I can't remain impartial in this research. My mother given to the vultures. After the wake by family members, which lasts five days, the undertaker carries on his back the corpse wrapped in a phula, a wool blanket, to a place where he will dispose of the body. Looking up, we see vultures waiting some ways off, with respect, it seems. A family member must stay to the end of the ritual. I believe Albert was the witness to the carving of my mother's body and to it being fed to the vultures that are sacred creatures here in Tibet.

The narration stops here.

Rachel rummages through the photos, bringing them closer to the yellow flame. The nude cadaver lies on its belly on a stone platform. Nearby burns a fire from which dense smoke rises. In a series of photos, the undertaker is dissecting the body, cutting the flesh in small pieces and heaping it to the side. In another series, he crushes the bones, mixing them with stampa, the local barley meal, as Jeanne has noted on the back of one snapshot, and forming this mixture into small balls. In several snapshots, in dozens more, the man feeds the vultures with the crushed barley-bone mixture, then with morsels of flesh.

Nausea rising, Rachel can't control the shaking of her hands. It is not the custom per se that troubles her. One custom is as good as another. It is this world in which she finds herself tonight and the fact that Jeanne has finally discovered the truth. Her dead mother, eaten by vultures. It is learning that her own father disappeared in a snowstorm, alone, in a far, faraway land. *Hima alaya*. Snow abode.

So, Jeanne called, Rachel came. Jeanne found her answer at last and died. And now, Rachel inherits a new burden made of her father's and her aunt's snapshots, films, audio recordings, written notes. Augmented by Jeanne's own observations. In her voice. Now mute.

Tell me, Jeanne, was the game worth the candle? Is the sacred game finally over? Will I be able to close this damn book once and for all?

With her baby finger, Rachel traces the white scar meandering across her forehead. Blows out the candle. Lies down on the straw mat. Tries to pierce the darkness pulsating in front of her eyes. She would pursue her mute dialogue with Jeanne, but the three high notes of the reed flute stop and a man of flesh and bones and hatred comes from another mountain to terrorize her. Stiff as a board, she listens.

The silence of the blue-black night shatters in an angry scream. The man roars. Above Rachel's head, the Nepalese woman answers. The man replies with a long argument full of rage. Fleas have found Rachel. In the dark, she glances toward her cousin, wondering if the vermin are also bothering her.

The woman comes down the narrow staircase and rushes outside. The man is right up against the house. A single vicious voice in the dark. A broken flute, carrying its distorted notes from mountain to mountain. The woman shrieks long and hard, syllables stretching into monotonous sounds.

The man bellows again, stronger, more menacing. That's it. He has come to claim Jeanne's body. You had a Nepalese lover, Jeanne? A Tibetan lover? The male claiming his due. Petrified on her mat, Rachel wonders why Rana doesn't take charge. The one coming down the stairs is not Rana, but his little brother. Rachel opens her eyes as wide as she can in an attempt to see in the dark. Nocturnal blindness makes her vulnerable. Disoriented, she can't find her lighter, her matches.

The boy opens the door. Rachel peeks outside. The night is less dark than inside the house. A flea walks on her belly, takes a bite. She squashes the insect. And fear, a true fright discharges from her belly as the man is standing on the threshold, not two steps from her face, a sickle in his hand. He stares at her, the white of his eyes alive, panicky.

The man's stocky body is squarely visible in the open doorway. He points a finger. At Jeanne? At Rachel? He screams. The woman shoves the raging man outside, pointing toward the living guest, pointing toward the dead guest, all the while shrieking. The man pushes his way back inside.

Fleas are still grazing on Rachel's flesh. Once more, the woman expels the man from her home. Tearing each other apart with their rage. The little brother half-closes the door, letting the paler night into the house. He moves into the shadows. Comes out. Armed with a knife. Rachel feels life trickling out of her. What if Jeanne was murdered in this house, her body thrown into a deep valley?

This night belongs to raw instinct. To trek through the mountains of Nepal, only to find Jeanne in ultimate stillness, never again to hear the three high notes of the reed flute, to die, her throat slit by a seven-year-old boy, to carry with the last moment of consciousness the screams, the terrible screams of a man and a woman consumed with hatred.

No. Rachel has not died. With fear and pride, the boy stands guard over her. The screams are getting more distant. Carrying a lamp made out of a tin can, the woman comes back. Pushes the door shut.

Rachel gets up. Where is Rana? She wants to leave Jeanne behind in her Nepalese death. Go far away from this place she does not understand.

Sleep, orders the woman.

Docile, Rachel lies down again. The woman goes back upstairs with her child. Once upstairs, she resumes the screaming match until her voice is raw. The man's voice reaches from afar, from the next mountain, as if the man had flown away on the wind. Soon, silence re-establishes itself. The fleas are voracious. The trek and her sorrow catch up with her. At last, Rachel sleeps.

▲ In the mud house filled with cold and congealed smoke, a blue dawn enters through cracks, pushing the shadows into corners. Somewhere, a cock crows. Where is the flute?

Outside, clouds shroud the land. Dewdrops drip from the roof. Inside, Rachel sits on her mat, her back to the villagers who have begun their daily chores, as if they had not witnessed the night's events. A neighbour comes in to fetch embers to rekindle her cooking fire.

A lump in her throat, her heart pounding, Rachel stares at the vaporous fabrics and at the yellow flowers that brighten the dawn. Slowly, she gets up and reaches toward the veils, remembering the horrible rigidity of Jeanne's arm she felt last night.

Closing her eyes, she pulls away the layers of thin fabric, holding them high so as not to touch her cousin. Still as a statue, she waits a few seconds. Then holding her breath, bracing for the shock, choking on saliva, she opens her eyes.

It is no longer Jeanne, that. And yet, at the beginning of the fall, it was her. When she hit the bottom of the cliff, nothing of her remained. Half her face is gone and what is left is a white yellow tumefaction. Part of the skull is visible where hair and skin were ripped under the impact with rock. Rachel replaces the shroud, rushes outside in the cold humid air, runs past the last house and sinks to the ground. She wails, letting it all out. No shame in tears and sobs, for what she has lost is irreparable. End game.

Later, people carry the pallet covered with fresh sprays of flowers. They walk toward the next village, deeper into the mountains. Rachel follows the funeral procession, inquiring about nothing.

When they reach the village, an old man dressed in saffron robes presides over the ceremony. A stone deity splattered with red dye occupies the centre of a small square. In front of that effigy has been built the pyre on top of which is laid the corpse with shroud and flowers. Small bells send crystalline sounds into the air. Secret words are recited, then the pyre is lit. The flames work easily on the layers of fabric, less so on the cadaver. Rachel shakes all over, terrified to see the mutilated face. But soon, the roaring blaze takes over everything.

Rachel looks up toward Borlang. A man standing on a knoll waves a sickle, staring with rage at the blaze.

Him crazy. Rana's mother pats Rachel's hand. Him crazy.

An hour later, the flames become less intense. The limbs have been burned, but the long bones, and the skull, and the carbonized trunk are still eerily solid. Where are those famous grey ashes to be scattered?

Rana, we must burn everything. Everything.

Wood is expensive, Miss Rachel.

Rachel gives him a thick wad of rupees: I want ashes. Only ashes, Rana.

Rana shows the money to the old man. The old man gives orders. Children bring more wood. Well-fed once more, the fire rekindles. Grows in intensity.

By late morning, it is over. Wood and corpse have been consumed. On the flagstones, a pile of ashes mixed with the brittle thigh bones and part of the skull. The old man crushes the bone fragments. Then, he stirs the ashes until they cool down enough to be handled. Rana scoops up the remains of his sister-in-spirit and lovingly drops them into a funeral urn. He presents the urn to Rachel. She accepts the jar. Presses her cousin to her heart. Tells Rana she is ready to go back down the mountain with the box of archives and the urn, both vessels filled with a past that will forever remain closed.

Touching her scar in a gesture of farewell, Rachel looks one last time at the square where a few hours ago a roaring wall of fire was burning and where, now, only a stone statue stands with a dispassionate face.

Assiniboine / Crossroads

DISCLAIMER

Let us be clear. Ours are not the horrendous
climbing stories you read in alpine journals and
other publications dedicated to *extreme* outdoor
pursuits. For mountains to have meaning in your
life, you don't have to be on the thirty-fifth pitch of a
Big Wall on Baffin Island in the middle of a blizzard
at −40°C, while Jake, still insisting on leading despite
frostbitten fingers, hammers a pin into crumbly
rock, while you, belaying on this pitch, haven't
slept a wink in three nights as you and your (crazy)
partner, anchored to the mountain two thousand
metres above the glacier and three hundred
kilometres from the nearest hamlet, are pummelled
by sleet then snow then wind, after having run
out of food two days ago with seven pitches still
ahead, including the horrible crux of the notorious
overhang with the unstable cornice you have to
tunnel through to gain the summit ridge, and
everyone knows the summit ridge ain't the *summit*
yet, and, right now, your mood is deteriorating
faster than the weather, from foul to murderous,
and you're nurturing wicked thoughts of cutting the
rope between you and fucking Jake who, once again,

talked you into climbing *another* goddam *remote* mountain, but while shivering and swearing, you also know that, if you survive this misery, after a shower, a meal, two twelve-hour rounds of sleep, when you're toasty in that pub guzzling your fifth beer, you'll be raving to everyone, whether they want to hear it or not, how flat-out *awesome* it is to climb rad routes with that son-of-a-bitch Jake. Not those kinds of stories. We don't want to lead you astray.

GIANNA & GREGOR

A SMALL OPENING

Not for the first time, we are contemplating the North Ridge of Mount Assiniboine, its edge sharpened in brilliant sunshine.

The North Ridge, a classic climb and the easiest route to reach the summit, offers advanced scrambling on sometimes loose rock, with short sections of fifth-class climbing. Located on the Great Divide, the 3,618-metre pyramid of grey limestone is the seventh highest peak in the Canadian Rockies and the highest mountain in the Southern Rockies. Assiniboine rises nearly 1,525 metres above Lake Magog. From the campground near the lake, you begin by hiking, then you scramble via a headwall, then up snow slopes to get to the moraine where the Hind Hut serves as an alpine refuge. Higher up, you face the ridge. Nine hundred metres to the summit. Not too difficult if the rock is free of ice and snow and if you don't get off route.

In human parlance, mountains quickly become a litany of facts. Oh but, there is more to them than statistics. We first saw the peak from the Sunshine Meadows, shortly after arriving in Calgary from the Far East. Over the years and from many vantage points, while hiking, scrambling, climbing, we kept seeing its distinctive shape profiled in the distance among many peaks. Mount Assiniboine, beckoning. Seventh highest peak, as in a

lucky number, perhaps. Rising on the Great Divide, as metaphor
for what our life together had never been. Spanning decades,
our relationship is defined by movement and an indefatigable
avoidance of the commonplace. We never have climbed the
mountain.

AT A CROSSROADS

Our desire to climb Assiniboine now is not a race against time.
Time that is left to us. Neither is it another exercise in checking
off yet another peak. This is an adjustment. Earlier this summer,
we reached two milestones. We both turned sixty-five (to say we
celebrated our birthdays would be a hyperbole) and we counted
forty years together.

GIANNA: Five years ago, might as well be five weeks ago, we
    turned sixty. I was flabbergasted how fast we reached that
    number. Took to my bed, remember?
GREGOR: Taking to your bed, you might as well take to your grave.
GIANNA: We are officially *senior* citizens. Senior! The age of
    the walker.

Our adjustment of what we've postponed for too long. As in
putting one's affairs in order before the Big Vanishing Act.
    We are here now. At long last. Early August, the height of
summer in this region of earth. The closest we've ever been to
the peak. An adjustment for all the times we couldn't make it.
For all the interruptions and interferences from work, life, the
weather. Why do we persist in thinking that, if we don't make the
summit tomorrow, there will be no take two? As it happens so
often with mountains, we try and if we have to bail, we try again.
Now though, we have to do it right the first time.
    Without the forest fires, this campground near Lake Magog
would be filled with hikers and climbers. And so would the
nearby Naiset Cabins. And not a few well-to-do climbers from

Europe or the States or Japan or China would be staying at the
swanky lodge and would hire the services of a personal guide.
The fires burning hectares of prime forest in Alberta and British
Columbia are our chance of making it without the crowd. Apart
from those fires, this summer has been a rare season of nothing
but high pressure.

Contemplating the North Ridge, we don't admit it, but we
are experiencing a bit of stage fright. At sixty-five, our bones
and sinews are not what they used to be. To say nothing of our
increasing slowness. We no longer have the energy of even a
decade ago. And the loss of physical strength is exponential.
The faster we lose it, the faster we will lose it, And mindset too
is a factor. Of late, we have been noticing a drop in our mental
resolve. Waning, our love of extravagance. Without it to boost
stamina, the smallest change in the complex alignment of stable
weather, good mountain conditions and minimal human traffic
risks turning us around. Neither one of us will be the first one to
suggest it. But it will come. With little resistance, we will pack
our bags and decamp. We and the mountains, at a crossroads.

REHEARSAL WITH THE INSECT PEOPLE

The evening before departure, we opened a bottle of wine. The
street light was casting a bright glow on the kitchen table. Felt as
if we were on stage. Assiniboine very much on our minds.

GIANNA, sipping her wine: Last night, I had a strange dream.
GREGOR: Not falling off Assiniboine, I hope?
GIANNA: The hordes were coming.
GREGOR: The hordes?
GIANNA: We were saying farewell and we were being pushed
    back by the hordes. Every hiking trail, every mountain face
    was teeming with people. Tiny people. Like crabs or bedbugs.
    Crawling everywhere.

GREGOR: Farewell? Farewell to what? The mountains?

GIANNA: Oh, I don't know. Farewell to love, maybe. To the *idea* and the *feel* of mountaineering. Silence, solitude...

GREGOR: Sheer terror too?

GIANNA: In the dream, nobody was pushing and shoving. It was all so *civilized*. And yet, it felt... like one of your nightmarish shadow puppets on the mountain face.

GREGOR, using the street light streaming on the back wall of the kitchen to create shadow shapes with his hands: Aye. I'll improvise a Rockies horror show out of your dream of the Insect People. Fire away.

GIANNA: More like the Human Zoo. Speaking of which, did you know? There was actually a zoo in Banff townsite in the 1920s.

GREGOR, hands forming a wapiti, morphing into the aquiline profile of a human face: Carving the heads of our most cherished politicians into the walls of Rundle, like the goofy Americans did on Rushmore. Imagine climbing the bridge of a nose. Negotiating the ledge system of the creases in a forehead. And you and I are part of the ever-expanding zoo.

GIANNA: I know that. Burning gas, logging thousands of kilometres on paved roads. I know that. And for what? To satisfy our selfish pleasure.

GREGOR: So, it wasn't all grim and gruesome, after all?

And his nimble hands tipped into a deer hit by a car.

GIANNA: What are you suggesting? From now on, we should walk all the way to the mountains? Each time?

GREGOR: Not go at all.

GIANNA: You wouldn't say that if you were in your twenties. Or fifties even.

GREGOR: Just knowing they are there should suffice.

GIANNA: Right, sure. And yet, tomorrow... Are we bailing?

GREGOR: As long as we keep driving to the mountains, even
using the outhouses provided, we are part of your hordes,
Gianna.

And his hands made a shadow man speaking from both sides of
his mouth.

GIANNA: Mr. Puppet Master playing devil's advocate! What
bothers me is... What if the great weather holds and...
GREGOR: We want the weather to hold.
GIANNA: And the North Ridge is crawling with climbers and
their guides?
GREGOR, making shadow insect: Crabs and bedbugs.
GIANNA: That's what my dream...
GREGOR: I don't like crowds on a climb any more than you. But
this is a crowded world. We'll adapt. Climb in turn with other
parties.
GIANNA: Climbers above will bomb us with rocks they dislodge.
Impatient hot shots will push us aside. I have visions of
disasters, tangled ropes, dropped tools.

And she took a gulp of wine.

GREGOR: Slow down. My hands can barely keep up with the
overload of disastrous scenes. Imagining the worst is hardly
useful.
GIANNA: Just rehearsing the climb. The city sure is creeping
into the mountains. We are at the crossroads, Gregor. We and
the mountains.
GREGOR, clapping his hands hard, ending the impromptu,
pouring himself a fresh glass of wine: Relax, Gia. The
mountains couldn't give a shit. Your hordes, and us of the

Insect People too, don't forget, are but a blip on their
geological clock. In any case, before your dream becomes
reality, we'll be long dead.

GIANNA: That is my wish.

BITTERSWEET

GIANNA: For me, the relationship was bittersweet. The love-
hate relationship, complicated. With Gregor? Not with
Gregor. Never with Gregor. With the mountains. The dos and
the don'ts. Acceptance and refusal. It took me a long time
to realize the tug-of-war was not between the mountains
and me, exactly. It was between my two physical selves. The
ambivalence generated by the active self (bitter) and the
passive self (sweet). Sure, I had been active, travelling and
walking, oh that, I had done in excess, but always in the
flats. Otherwise, I had never leaned toward all-out physical
activities, like *sports*. But Gregor tried to convince me
mountaineering was not a sport. Mountaineering was a
state of mind.

State of mind? When I create my wild headdresses and
perform his stories on stage, I told him, my state of mind
is activated plenty enough. And so is his, he said, doing
shadowgraphy. That was not in question. But he still insisted
mountains were a state of mind. Although I teased him,
they're rocks, Greggy, only rocks, I started to feel in the body
that those rocks could play tricks with your head.

But when he went on to say that, with age, the blood of
imagination thins out and becomes anemic, and mountains
oxygenate imagination better than our workshop or the stage,
I wondered about his state of mind. Still. I couldn't contradict
him when he pointed out the body was built for walking,
not to be forced into a chair. Walking, yes, I agreed. But did
it have to be vertical walking? I was not a squirrel scratching

its way up a tree. Gregor was unfazed and recommended patience, because it takes time and effort to break the addiction of the chair.

The addiction of the chair. In the great stifling humidity of the Far East, we had nurtured the passive self (sweet). Lounging in lounge chairs. But here? This region of unpredictable seasons was reactivating our desire for movement. Greg insisted our active selves (bitter) were calling us, loud and clear.

He warned me. With my ass on my chair, my love of movement was fast going to seed. Before my time, I'd transform into a matron of the commonplace. And his hands formed the shadow of an old woman in her rocking chair.

That was shock therapy. Gregor jolting my active self. Often, at his risk and peril. He proposed a mountain. I glared at him. Not wanting to go. And yet, not wanting to miss out. I went. Reluctantly. Dragging my ass, cursing the incline. Passive self pining for that chair. On every hike, the repetition of pain in muscles and lungs seemed pointless. Masochistic, even. I cursed his pig-headedness. Pig-headed, aye, he admitted that much. Necessary pig-headedness to counteract the insignificance triggered by idleness. The chair, Gia, he said. Beware of the chair.

Gregor and his chair. That was a laugh. Over time though, I came to appreciate his pluck for prying me out of my chair at his risk and peril.

In the early days, I often gave up, sometimes fifty metres below the summit. He didn't get it. A few more minutes, I'd stand on the top. Why come all that way and stop now?

For the day to be complete, he had to stand on the summit. For me, the top—the *peak-bagger* syndrome—did not matter. I'd had my fill and that was that. He went on ahead by himself. I waited in sunshine or in wind, sprawled on my pack, quieting my breath. Listening to the layers of silence. That too had to be experienced. The depth of silence, rising in layers around me. I was content. And maybe disappointed with myself. And he came back down with another summit under his belt. He was happy. A little sad we had not summited together. And, together, we returned home. The long, long way home.

THE MAN FROM MARYLAND

GREGOR: From the pass, Gia and I watched his progress through the scree. A small lone figure slipping and sliding up the steep rocky slope. Stopping often to catch his breath. To look up and assess the end of the ordeal. Never once turning around to look back and study the land as it would appear on the way down. Resolute, he resumed scrambling. The hiker made it to the pass. Grinned from ear to ear. To show courage. To hide exhaustion. He walked toward us. An American, it turned out. From Maryland, he told us.

The man from Maryland had no problem following the trail in the woods. But it was impossible to find the trail in the rubble, he said, taking off his small daypack and reaching for a bottle of Coke.

I played mountain teacher, as on stage I had fascinated spectators with my shadow hands shaped into an old couple mating. Once on the scree, there are no human-made trails. Only occasionally tracks the Rocky Mountain sheep make for themselves. Those tracks go where the sheep want to go, not where people want to go. The sheep are searching for food, for water. Scramblers are aiming for the summit. So, on scree, you must pick your way through the rocks, finding the places where the rubble is most stable.

The man from Maryland was perplexed. No one had informed him about that. He wanted to know where the rock was more stable. Even suggested signs should be posted to indicate where to go. Otherwise, people could get lost. And if there were signs to tell you where the rubble is more stable, it might prevent injury.

I was watching Gia, expecting a snide remark. But she kept quiet. Gianna of lost words in the mountains, preferring to let me do the talking. Instead, she grazed on the distance. Watching the man from Maryland drink his Coke, I wanted to tell him that scrambling was an acquired skill, like an acquired taste.

But he was expostulating about the boundless American genius building paved roads up fairly high mountains. High enough that, nearing the summit, car radiators used to boil over routinely; motors stalled. If the Canadians were not up to the task, and he didn't mean any disrespect, at least, surely, signs in the rubble would save time and energy. And it'd be easier.

Easier? I couldn't resist tripping him up. Why come to these mountains? They have wild mountains in the US too. The man from Maryland acknowledged the fact with great pride, as if their peaks had been built by their Corps of Engineers. But he had read online the Canadian Rockies were less crowded than the European Alps and the Rockies in the States. He was after the real *wilderness* experience.

And so, did the man from Maryland enjoy the scramble? Did the place live up to his expectations? He swore it did. Told me he was a cardiologist. This place restored heart and spirit. This spectacular landscape. Uncrowded. We were the first people he had encountered *all day*.

I spoke in as kind a Canadian voice as I could, pointing out, if there were signs everywhere to make his scramble easier, it wouldn't be the same unspoiled, uncrowded place he enjoyed so much, now, would it?

Caught in his faulty argument, the man from Maryland nodded. And stared at what he and scores of others still referred to as the *landscape*. And proceeded to shoot the land *systematically*. I knew he would post those photos online, with a detailed description of where in the *wilderness* his unspoiled experience had taken place.

Gia and I walked a little ways off. Had lunch. Waited until the man from Maryland started scrambling back down. I enjoyed watching that urbanized, educated man get smaller and smaller as he picked his way through the scree. A lone human form in our still (relatively) unspoiled mountains.

LOOKING BACK

When scrambling, from time to time, turn around. Study the land as it will appear on the way back down. Commit distinctive features to memory. You must know that the up and the down don't have the same aspect at all. You would be surprised how different the land looks on the way down and how easily it could confuse you. This morning, did we contour that outcrop? Is this the gully we took on the way up? Or was it that one? Careful. One of them we avoided because of cliffs.

On the way up, the land in your face is foreshortened. You see it in close-ups. You spot a spider scurrying between stones. Kinnikinnik growing close to the ground. Juniper shrubs sending green pollen into the air when you brush against their branches. A fossil revealed inside a stone cleaved by the action of freeze and thaw.

On the way down, the whole land is splayed out in front of you. You see the sheer magnitude of it. Rock faces shooting straight up from the valley floor. Twisted syncline. On your left, a long drop and on your right, disappearing from view, the ledge system you must negotiate to reach the alpine meadows lower down. Or the endless boulders precariously stacked, over which you must descend with half-bent knees, your weight resting on your quads. And still in front of you, several kilometres of incline before you reach the car.

THE INCLINE

GIANNA: I began tentatively. Said it was the incline. Wondered if I was *inclined* to engage in mountaineering. Despite Gregor's tireless incitement. The incline, I discovered, is an amazing thing. It seizes up your butt; it saws across your quads; it triggers cramps in your calf muscles. The incline shatters your knees and mashes the soles of your feet. Pumps masses of blood into your extremities. The incline cuts deep into your lungs. Grips your resolve and crushes it. The incline is more raw than the coldest day of winter. And it plays dangerous games with your head. Makes you angry. Nasty to your partner. Brings you to the verge of tears when you think the end is in sight, but it turns out there is more incline ahead; way more.

In the early years, Gregor would often assess, with confidence, that we were ten minutes from the summit. Relieved, grateful, I believed him with all my heart. But he was wrong. Again, the incline fooled us. Eventually, I learned to ignore his affirmations. Tackled the incline with grim surrender, stopping short of calling him a liar.

One season, the incline caught up with me and reactivated my childhood asthma. The perfect excuse to abandon the activity.

We had met on another incline in the Far East. Ah, those wild days when I was a wig maker in Hong Kong! Mixing Peking opera and Western contemporary performance art, our opera company was preparing a new production of Baucis and Philemon when Gregor happened to be passing through. As a

young shadowgrapher, he was offered a gig. We met backstage
and ours was an operatic romance. I still see us, Gregor, the
Scot with the gruff voice of fatalism and the mesmerizing
hands, and me with my Italian genes, which I used to full effect
in the best tradition of the tragi-comic. We milked our theatrical
selves for all it was worth and we made a roaring good time
of it. Then, the heat and the crowds of the Far East got the
better of us. We came to Canada to discover ice, to borrow a
phrase. I with a suitcase stuffed with stunning hairpieces, but
renting them out would not pay the bills. And Gregor with his
marketable hands, yes, but how many birthday parties can
you book to amuse kids with shadow figures of galloping
horses and leaping rabbits when they have video games
instead? Of course, we found jobs, we adapted, even if the
road was rocky for a while.

Now, with my asthma reactivated, Gregor would have to
find other partners. It had been so simple for me to be his
perpetual mountain buddy, as in the days of spectacular wigs
and baffling finger tricks. Or he would have to go by himself.
But I would not be happy for him to enter the hills alone. Solo
shows have their pitfalls. The potential for a freak accident or
an encounter with a bear would make me uneasy, back home.
(The *wife* wringing her hands, eyes on the clock.) But there
was more than those considerations.

We had been sharing adventures on and off stage for a
long time. We had never been the kind of couple to engage
in separate activities. If we did, it would have caused a rift
in the deep rapport that always existed between us. And
although I would be relieved to be relieved of my mountain
duty, I wanted the adventure. The being there together, in full
exertion mode, enduring the elements, being in the grip of
the incline, testing exposure. Breathing together this amazing
air. And what about afterward, reminiscing and sharing,

which translate into complete understanding? That would be lost if I stopped going.

So, I took a shallow breath, then a deeper breath and, week after week, I went grudgingly. October would bring the hiking season to an end. And then, in town, began the season of dinner parties with friends. I put away hiking boots and backpack until June. And forgot about the incline.

VERTIGO

GREGOR: As for me, I was hooked from the start. Rearing to go, I wanted to try it all. Began by buying *The Canadian Rockies Trail Guide* and, later, *Kananaskis Country Trail Guide*. The former was the hiking bible in an era of few guidebooks and no Internet. Hiking was fine. It became necessary.

I still performed shadowgraphy on home and out-of-town stages, in shows with or without Gianna. Also, I was now a bookbinder and restorer, as had been my grandfather in Edinburgh. I loved, and still love, the tools and the smell of old leather and the broken spines of damaged books. Though fine, the workshop was too confining a place.

So, every week, I pored over the guidebooks, suggested this hike and that hike. Gianna bought me topo maps as birthday gifts. One year, I wrapped two mountaineering axes and placed them under the Christmas tree.

Late June, sometimes early July, signalled the opening of the hiking season and the season of blisters, though the blisters never stopped us from going out once a week until mid-fall. It took us a number of years to realize our boots, too tight, were the source of the misery. Before each hike, Gianna went through the ritual of applying moleskin to all the contact points on her feet. I didn't think I needed any and, later on the hike, grimly endured my bleeding blisters.

With each new hiking season, we chose trails that were more involved in distance and difficulty. Until one day, when I came face to face with vertigo. I had never had it. Why should I have vertigo now?

That day, a short section of the trail hugged a rock face on our left and was exposed on the right until, further along, the trail widened again. I denied the issue. Tried to step forward. Could go no further. Was frustrated; pushed myself to go on; no wuss; then had to admit defeat. How could that happen?

Gianna suggested vertigo lived in the mountains. Could she go on? She hesitated; said yes. I could see she was trying to spare my feelings. That made it worse. She pretended vertigo was like allergies. Some develop it, others don't. Great! That made me feel a whole lot better.

I was embarrassed, Gianna could see that plainly enough, but I could tell she was not disappointed. In those early days, turning back was never an issue for her. What had become an issue was my vertigo. It had to be dealt with. As had her asthma. We managed to control both. The only way to conquer vertigo and asthma was by not giving up, was by not giving in. You keep trying.

We tested our limits and began scrambling. Endured endless scree. Tackled snow slopes. Learned to self-arrest with mountaineering axes and practised tumbling down low-angled snow slopes without stabbing ourselves with the picks. We enjoyed ridge walking. Bought more specialized guidebooks and climbing equipment. Pairs of crampons were wrapped and put under the Christmas tree. We taught ourselves to climb on rock, first at sport climbing areas, then on more secluded multi-pitch climbs. Learned to travel roped up across glaciers. Practised crevasse rescue. Began climbing glaciated mountains, such as Mount Athabasca, Mount Joffre, the President. Many more mountains. Stretched the summer hiking and scrambling season to year-round mountaineering by adding ice climbing. And in our own way and in our own time, we dealt with the incline and vertigo. Like a well-rehearsed piece of theatre—no matter how foreboding at first—that shines on opening night. Until the incline became second nature, with or without exposure.

And through it all, in the distance, in sun or rain, in clouds or snow, the persistence of Mount Assiniboine.

GETTING PSYCHED UP

We set the camp stove on a flat stone on the ground.

GREGOR: I'll prime it. Get the fire going.
GIANNA, picking up the pot: I'll fetch water from that spigot.

Spigot seems a luxury. Usually, you get water directly from a creek or at the edge of a lake. In this British Columbia provincial park, a pipe must have been installed to run from Lake Magog to the campground to save campers the short steps to the lake.

GIANNA, carrying her pot of water, retrieving the food bag from the safety of the metal cache, returning to the campsite with a steady pace: I know the place's deserted, but I feel the hordes jostling at my back.

Waiting for the water to boil, we can't take our eyes off Assiniboine.

GREGOR: At least, doesn't look like we'll be bombarded by too many climbers.
GIANNA: How long to the hut, do you figure?

GREGOR: Let's see. The trail around the lake, then scree to the headwall, then scramble up ledges.

GIANNA: The Gmoser Highway.

GREGOR: Aye. Then snow slopes to the refuge. People do it in two or three hours.

GIANNA: Seems a lot farther to me than a couple of hours from here. And I bet we'll be slower.

GREGOR: And if we don't go off route. There may be routefinding.

GIANNA: I'm more concerned about the North Ridge itself.

GREGOR: For what I've read, better to avoid the gullies and stay on firmer rock. From the refuge, there are cairns in the scree, then a black rock band and, after that, a red band. From there, we regain the ridge up a grey band. Good holds. And there are fixed pitons. That's good.

GIANNA: Right! The actual climbing. Fifth-class rock bands. Hope we don't go off route.

GREGOR: We have to stay below the cornice. Then the final ridge to the summit.

GIANNA: Reading about it, always seems straightforward, doesn't it? Until you have rock right in your face.

GREGOR: We just have to pierce the rock bands in the right places and know where to penetrate the ridge with the good holds. We'll be fine.

GIANNA: *Pierce? Penetrate?* Sounds like war up there. Like B Company being slaughtered trying to secure Hill of Beans.

GREGOR, scrutinizing the big rock: We may luck out and have the whole mountain to ourselves. We descend the same way. Only a couple of rappels. Maybe three. At least, we have dry conditions. Apparently, it's a lot more entertaining when downclimbing in wet or icy conditions.

GIANNA: It'll take us forever. But I'm up to the challenge. I think.

GREGOR: Most people do it in eight to eleven hours return. But it'll take us longer. That's why we'll stay at the refuge overnight.

GIANNA: Good plan. We'll scramble back down the next morning. We'll leave the tent set up here. I don't see the point of taking it down and storing it with the extra food while we're gone. Doesn't look like the place will have much traffic in our absence.

GREGOR: You're really up to it?

GIANNA: Psyching myself up.

BACK TO COMFORT

We sit recalling the middle years, cockier times when we disappeared into the hills for days. Camping in the backcountry, climbing one peak after another, moving to the next camping area. Sometimes, camping out of bounds.

GIANNA: Remember that time, how wary I was of moose trampling us on their early morning wanderings? I was convinced we'd erected the tent on an ancient moose byway.

Camping, climbing. Decamping, hiking out, setting up camp elsewhere. Climbing, decamping. Walking out.

Your rhythm, your outlook, your muscles, your face, absolutely everything about you as it never is in the city. As it never was on stage.

GREGOR: Even when I was showing entire narratives in shadows with my hands, and while you, dressed up wig and all, as you were, moved across centre stage. Nothing compared. And we were not trampled by any moose.

They were not comfortable, those camping-climbing trips. Nothing cozy, those nights in the tent, sleeping on the ground. But what you gain more than makes up for what you lose in comfort. No sound, unless it is raining. Or, if you are camping near a glaciated mountain, the occasional thunder of an avalanche or a rock slide. Or the ripple of a creek if you camp beside one. Or the wind howling if you set up your tent on a ridge. Otherwise, a deep quiet prevails. And the animals in the north country are soundless. Nothing like in the steam bath of the Far East where the cries of nocturnal animals are a continuous racket.

GIANNA: It didn't stop me from being nervous. Always an ear on the potential encounter with other campers. Never knowing to what subspecies of *Homo sapiens* they belonged. Were they the seekers of silence as we were? Or were they the noisemakers of the party animal subspecies, believing camping in the backcountry was an extension of the mall culture?

GREGOR: Think about the many times we mounted mini expeditions into solitude. Entered deserted campsites. The whole place to ourselves. Save for a lone caribou feeding at the edge of the forest. Or as we fetched water from a creek, being watched by the quiet mule deer.

Camping in the backcountry has nothing in common with camping by your car, or in your behemoth RV. And camping in the backcountry has nothing to do with comfort. When you have to carry everything on your back over long and arduous distances, you choose carefully what to bring. Comfort we will always have when returning to the city.

GREGOR: Unless we lose it all and become street people. But then, we'd rather live grim and gruesome in some badly insulated cabin in the mountains.

GIANNA: That's your way of creating your own world within a world on the verge of disappearing?

GREGOR: The badly insulated cabin in the mountains would be a last *resort*. Ha! But think about it. Comfort is at its best after a day spent in the cold, ice climbing or snowshoeing. Or days of exertion backpacking and climbing.

Even the unassuming day trips deliver their moments. The whiteouts. The going off route. Scrambling back down on rock coated with verglas. Neither of us liking it one bit, but resolutely descending. Focusing on the moment that could change everything with one misstep. The four-hour scramble that begins on a sunny summer morning, stretching into the night to a seventeen-hour epic. There are such days, and they can happen an hour's drive from Calgary on a relatively small mountain.

Back to comfort, talking up a storm. Doing the post-mortem. Watching the tempest, still so real in our minds, relief and excitement printed on our windburned faces. Together, building story, across time and across silences.

Back to comfort then acquires a whole new meaning when you bear the land deep in the bone.

THE CHECKLIST

In the beginning, the reflex was to make a list of mountains to climb. After each outing, to check off the mountain climbed that day.

If fatigue or a sudden thunderstorm interfered, usually near the summit, the mountain could not be checked off. It had to be done again. And from scratch, since you cannot resume from the point where you had to turn back. We braced ourselves. All that trouble just to get to the point where we turned back. Were we in better shape today? Would that blue sky remain blue for the next twelve hours? Any puff of cloud getting puffier or weakness in our resolve when we wasted time going up a gully that ended nowhere and we had to backtrack could be signs we might fail to make the summit. And then, and then... we would have to come back again and again. In the beginning, a chore, an ordeal. A discouragement.

GIANNA: What was it with this list thing? The grocery list of mountain climbing? The job jar of domestica, like washing the kitchen floor or doing laundry? Was climbing as many peaks in a season a duty? A domestic duty? Collecting trophies?

Nevertheless. We greeted days that had been long and hard. Days when routefinding among rock spires and gullies had meant detours, side-hilling, losing elevation only to regain it. Days when we stood on the hard-earned summit and when we contemplated the work still ahead that had to be done in reverse, because standing on top was only a half-done job. Some days, you scrambled down forever; tedious work. Other days, you had to set up rappels and had to be doubly attentive, aware of mistakes from fatigue. Though if anything brings a state of happiness, it is the lightness of rappelling. When you leave the edge and let yourself slide along the rope into the void.

On those wondrous days, when the climb was no longer at the back of our minds where it had lain semi-dormant for seasons, sometimes for years, at last, we felt a peculiar release. The mix of mission accomplished and physical and mental fatigue made us giddy.

GREGOR: Back home, it was my job to turn on the gooseneck lamp and set up the white screen.

GIANNA: And although I was dead tired, I never *tired* of watching
your hands form, dissolve and reform the mountain du jour
in shadow. And with this sleight of hand, the mountain
disappeared from our minds.

GREGOR: And we'd fall asleep in a cold second.

GIANNA: No nightmare about invading hordes!

Side by side in our usual bed, we rappelled into the dreamless
night.

GREGOR: And next morning, I'd relish in making that simple
flick of the pencil next to the peak in question on my long list
of mountains. ✓

IN A NAME

Sipping tea and munching on dried fruit. Musing about
Assiniboine.

GREGOR: In the 1880s, geologist George Dawson named the
mountain for the Indians who hunted in this area.

GIANNA: Good for him! Someone who didn't saddle yet another
peak with the name of some minister. Or a war ship.

GREGOR: But Assiniboine ended up with the sobriquet
Matterhorn of the Rockies. And only because the shape of our
mountain resembles that one.

GIANNA: Okay, then. Why Matterhorn? Why not mont Cervin
des Rocheuses? Or Monte Cervino? That would have pleased
my Italian grandmama. That poor mountain is nothing but a
confusion of names, with its base straddling Switzerland and
Italy. Identity crisis.

GREGOR: Don't you know? The mountain has to be politically
correct to satisfy three languages and save face, all of its stony
faces. A geological fact, Gia. Ask Dawson. It's all Whymper's fault.

GIANNA: Whymper?

GREGOR: When he climbed from the Swiss side. 1865. July 14.

GIANNA: Bastille Day! I bet the French were jealous. I didn't
know you had such a head for dates.

GREGOR: Eh! I dated you!

GIANNA: And so, the name was forced on our Assiniboine.

GREGOR: Years later, when he was sixty-one or so, Whymper
heard about our *Matterhorn* and couldn't resist coming over
to claim first ascent.

GIANNA: Sixty-one! And here we are, sixty-five. Don't tell me he
didn't make it.

GREGOR: Waited too long.

GIANNA: Tomorrow, will we fail too, because of age? Still, with
the two or three guides he'd have had in those days, he stood
a good chance of summiting. Maybe we should have hired a
guide.

GREGOR: Not a chance. The star climber had gone to seed.
Dipsomaniac, he was.

GIANNA: Too boozy to climb? What a wimp, Whymper!

GREGOR: Who knows. Maybe the Assiniboine, on a break from
hunting, found time to draw some caricatures of him. An
image in rock, of the staggering white man losing face.

MILESTONE

We stowed the food in the metal cache and are taking the
climbing gear from our packs and dumping it into the tent,
keeping only a few items for the hike. Walking in the opposite
direction, we turn our backs on Assiniboine; that is for tomorrow.

GREGOR, aside: Youth is no guarantee of success. In 1978, Gia
and I moved to Calgary. That summer, we hiked into the
Sunshine Meadows and saw Assiniboine for the first time.
There appeared to be a storm over the summit. But being

green as hell about mountains, we knew nothing about climbing. Months later, by chance, I came across the obituary.

Bugs McKeith died as he was coming down Assiniboine in a storm. He was thirty-three. Was considered one of the leading star climbers in his home country of Scotland. Eventually, he emigrated to Canada in the early 1970s. Made many great ascents all over North America. His death hit me hard. A fellow Scot. Of my generation too. What kept going round in my head was that, maybe, he died the very same day we watched the cloud-clapped mountain. If we'd had eagle eyes, if we'd had the ability to shrink distance and elevation, if we could have seen through stormy clouds, we might have seen him fall to his death.

The image stayed with me a long time. I created a memorial shadowgraphy of the accident. In August of the following year, in prime hiking season, I travelled to my native Edinburgh to perform the show at The Fringe. Gia and I realized then that plenty was happening, hidden from us. This mountaineering thing seemed to play in shadows, against the bright lights of the city. In the days before it became mainstream. Suburbanized, like tattoos. As we hike up a bluff so as not waste this day, it's all coming back to me.

GREGOR, clearing his throat: Remember Bugs McKeith?

GIANNA: Who? Oh, yes. Yes. Wasn't it his death, in a way, that triggered our interest in the mountains? I mean...

GREGOR: Aye, one gone, another, or two others ready to take his place.

GIANNA: A bit macabre. And spooky too, considering tomorrow.

GREGOR: Our arrival and his departure.

FUTURE INTERRUPTED

GIANNA: Sharing regrets? Why so gloomy on such a beautiful day?

GREGOR, laughing: Gloom too must be shared. And the pressure of work. Remember your big wig gig in Milano?

GIANNA: That was years ago! What about your escapade to Edinburgh?

GREGOR: I was gone a mere ten days. Besides, we weren't really doing anything in the mountains then. But Milan! It ruined an entire summer of climbing.

GIANNA: What an opportunity that was! Wigs for La Scala! For an entire opera season. And it got me more contracts. Opportunities, Greggy, we couldn't afford to miss.

GREGOR: You away! Any other time of the year, aye. But summers? Summers here are so precious.

GIANNA, aside: And so, Gregor did climb without me. Found good guys to partner with him. But it was not the same. Felt like a divorce. I in Milano making wigs. Gregor in the Rockies climbing Lefroy with good guys. Where was the sharing?

Not to be downcast. I did come back from Milan. And there would always be next year. And next year was a rainy summer. Next year would be better. We would climb Victoria together. We even considered Robson. At least, an outlier of Robson.

And then, there was life in the flats. *Opportunities* kept interrupting the rhythm of mountaineering. We postponed the biggies. There would always be next year. And next year and next year, and next year. Victoria kept eluding us. And so did Assiniboine. And next year kept passing us by.

Summers of continuous high pressure are so rare. Even when one materializes, it can be ruined in a twenty-minute downpour. A downpour in the valley translates into a snowstorm on a mountain. Summer snow not consolidated.

Danger of avalanche. Then, the sun melts the new snow that lower overnight temperature turns into verglas coating the rock face. The guides recommend against going up under such adverse conditions. You go without a guide. You take your chances. Sometimes, you don't come back.

GIANNA, clear-eyed again: Yes, our precious summers. Well, here we are, Greggy.

GREGOR: Aye. And tomorrow. It's now or never.

GIANNA: Because time, and crowds, don't forget, will put an end to everything. One year, next year will not come.

WEATHER

Our gloom session has put bounce into our step. We are coming back to camp properly oxygenated. Ready for the climb. We are redoing our packs for tomorrow. Reloading the climbing gear. In the morning, we will only have to add our sleeping bags and food for a couple of days. There are mattresses, stoves and dishes at the refuge; our packs will be relatively light. Relatively.

And then, something catches our eye. Something in the air makes us shiver. A change in atmospheric pressure? We both look up at the sky.

Meteorological transformation stops our packing and enthusiasm. Clouds bubbling, black as coal seams and tinged green and purple. Talk about the sudden reversal. How operatic of nature! Wind rising, wild. We check the moorings of tent and tarp. Bring gear and packs under the shelter of the tarp.

All at once, the deluge. Raindrops hit hard as tacks. Leave craters in the loose soil before ricocheting off the ground. Then in rapid succession, it hails and it snows. The mountain has vanished. Sleet accumulates on the tarp, causing it to sag. The tent may not withstand the storm. Before our entire sheltering system collapses, we must tighten the lengths of cord.

Donning rain pants and jackets, securing the hoods around our faces, we set to work. Untying and retying cords around rough tree trunks. Brushing mushy snow off the tarp as fast as the clouds discharge it. Checking that sleet and water roll off freely to the ground. With the adze of our mountaineering axes, we dig a narrow trench around the tent to divert the water that is now flowing downhill in rivulets. We can't see two paces in front of us. We are shadow shapes to each other.

And the sound-and-light show begins. Lightning so bright, it brings back the summer afternoon. Thunder so loud, it will burst our eardrums. Nature falling apart at the seams of its own extremes.

Back under the relative shelter of the tarp, we take a peek at the invisible mountain. Imagine ourselves stranded on the rock face, battered by the elements. Clinging to stone, expecting to be electrocuted with each bolt of lighting. When you can, you dump gear, throwing metal away from you. When you can.

As we did the time we were scrambling up the ridge of Gap Peak, just as the thunderhead exploded on top of us. Our saving grace was that we could drop down into the scree. The air was so charged with static electricity, our hair stood on end. And we heard the crackling sound of static and felt tingling on our skin.

Watching this storm, we play the game of ifs. If we had arrived at Lake Magog yesterday and if we had gone up the mountain this morning instead of tomorrow, at this hour, end of afternoon, we would be back in the shelter of the alpine hut. And, at that altitude, we would be watching a whiteout. Which means we would have summited in sunshine. The peak done, at last. Unless, we'd have been very slow and, in the tempest, we'd have had to bail. Doing those many rappels in bad weather. Caught in the terror of downclimbing on slippery rocks.

GREGOR: It almost happened to James Outram, the Scottish upstart.

GIANNA: Another Scot!

GREGOR, laughing: We do get around, don't we? In September 1901, Outram and his *two* Swiss guides made the first recorded successful climb of Assiniboine.

GIANNA: Ha! They checkmated the Inglese Whymper! Hurrah for the Scots!

GREGOR: Outram and his guides reached the summit via the southwest face. Instead of coming down the same way and against the guides' advice, he insisted to come down via what's now known as the North Ridge. They made it back in the nick of time. The next day, it snowed.

GIANNA: Lucky pig-headed Outram! His double luck must have made Whymper doubly pissed off. The bigwig in his day. And now, at the outer rim of his life, he couldn't bag his Matterhorn of the Rockies.

Watching rain and sleet, Assiniboine hidden behind a curtain of clouds, we are down here. Not up there. And tomorrow, the mountain will be encased in verglas. Our hearts sink. So close and yet so far.

PERFORMANCE

The meteorological lashing lasts until six o'clock. At six, it stops as suddenly as it had begun. All around us, intense dripping. Like the last tears after the hurt is gone. The clouds tear and dissipate. Summer brightness returns. The rain has penetrated the deepest recesses of the forest. Tree trunks shine black, soaked under their thick canopy. We presume no animal could find adequate shelter. At the moment, deer and squirrels, grizzlies and whiskey jacks are shaking off fur and feathers. A bird is actually trilling.

We leave the protection of the tarp, stepping in mud churned into psychedelic patterns. Mount Assiniboine is plastered.

GIANNA: The glaze will melt.

GREGOR: Dream on.

GIANNA: These are still the hot days of summer.

GREGOR: High up, the nights are cold.

GIANNA: *If* the daytime temperature stays warm and *if* it remains sunny, the sun will melt snow and verglas.

GREGOR: Oh, I don't know. We may still do it in our seventies.

GIANNA: The longer you wait, the thicker the crowd.

GREGOR: Or in our eighties.

GIANNA: Dream on.

GREGOR: You know Ulrich Inderbinen?

GIANNA: One of the guys with whom you climbed Lefroy while I was in Milano *ruining* your summer?

GREGOR: A Swiss mountain guide from Zermatt. He was 103 when he died in 2004.

GIANNA: There's hope for us, then. That's what you're saying?

GREGOR: He first climbed the Matterhorn, the real one, in 1921 and, a year later, he became a guide. He's said to have climbed the peak some 370 times.

GIANNA: And he survived all those climbs? Amazing. Still. Climbing our Assiniboine once will be plenty enough for me. But 370 times! It's like those stage actors who do a thousand performances of detective Gum Shoe. I always go for limited engagements.

GREGOR: Maybe he needed the money. Like your actor playing the detective.

GIANNA: Repetition takes the excitement out of doing what you're doing.

GREGOR: Inderbinen must have liked *performing* the Matterhorn. Apparently, he made his last ascent at ninety. And he retired from guiding at ninety-five.

GIANNA: What a guy!

We laugh.

GREGOR: The point is, climbing in our seventies or even in our eighties may not be far-fetched. If, unlike Whymper, we stay off the sauce.

GIANNA: Too late for that. Besides, why wait that long? We have enough food. Let's stay a couple more days. See what happens. I have a feeling we may still bag this peak.

HAUTE CUISINE

We have an early supper. Walk through the deserted campground to the metal cache to retrieve the food bag.

Water devastation everywhere. Soon enough, the thin soil will absorb the moisture. Can these mountains absorb human infestation too?

The sun is already evaporating water that has not yet seeped underground. A thick layer of fog hangs over Lake Magog. We are as landowners surveying the damage, quite alone in a campground that, at this time of year, should be crowded. Guests staying at the swanky Mount Assiniboine Lodge helicopter to the park, whereas most campers hike up the thirty or so kilometres, depending on the chosen approach. This summer of vast forest fires, the backcountry trails have been closed for weeks, hence the unusual lack of activity in the campground.

We too have flown in with our camping and climbing gear. We too are part of the invasion. And soon enough, we will decamp, walk the kilometre and a half to the lodge, en route to the helipad. In no time, we will be back in Calgary in the midst of traffic and leaf blowers.

At the moment, we selfishly overdose on the three powerful Ss of solitude, silence, stillness. For us, the deeper point of mountaineering. No chorus line, only this pas de deux.

The white gas hisses through the blue flame of the stove we have set again on the flat stone on the ground. As rocks and fallen logs are soaking wet, we will eat standing up, tucking away our dehydrated rehydrated elastic bands and Spackle, tonight's delight disguised as beef rotini or chicken primavera. We stand on either side of the stove, watching the pot.

Watching the pot, we conjure up the Assiniboine. A clever people.

Before the white men came with their chattel of metal, the Assiniboine had no cooking pots. So at dinnertime, they dug a hole in the ground they lined with a bison hide. They filled that ingenious pot with water, while they heated stones in a campfire nearby. Then they dropped the hot stones into the pot and added whatever food they wanted to cook. That's a capital invention. No pot to wash after dinner! If we can't always avoid the chore at home, at least when camping we do. By pouring the required amount of boiling water into the pouch of dehydrated food to rehydrate and warm it, and by setting the pouch into the pot of remaining water to complete the cooking process, we save ourselves the hassle of cleaning a dirty pot. How Assiniboine of us.

GIANNA: Yes, it's this cooking style of theirs that made people call them stone boilers, Stoney. Did you know that?

GREGOR: And so, the Stoney and the Assiniboine are one and the same people?

GIANNA: Like the Matterhorn/Cervin/Cervino in Europe, the mountain with too many names.

Our cache of mountain trivia. The crumbs of history sticking to mind, as bits of food lodged between teeth. At moments like tonight, the tidbits we manage to dislodge from a recessed memory lobe with mental floss.

GIANNA: How much of the tidbits of our lifetime together will still float through our memory in the years to come? Will we go blank? Be desiccated minds?

GREGOR: What dehydrated delight will we share tonight?

ANIMAL MYSTIQUE

In our tent after the storm. A sense of loss. Staring down into the dark tunnel of old age.

GREGOR: Okay, showtime! To lighten the mood. Wear your headlamp and shine the beam on the wall of the tent. Good.

And he forms his hands into the shadow of a grizzly bear rooting.

GIANNA: Is the official transformation of the mountains to accommodate the hordes sufficient cause for us to end it all?

The bear on the wall raises its head. Sniffs the air. Stands on its hind legs. Readies itself for the attack.

GREGOR: You mean a double suicide?

GIANNA: I mean for us to hang not ourselves, but our packs and climbing ropes.

GREGOR: And exchange them for what? A time-share in Cancun or Palm Springs?

GIANNA: To escape our harsh, unending winter.

GREGOR: What? No more ice climbing?

GIANNA: We're sixty-five. Our future has never been so close to our present.

The shadow bear vanishes from the beam of light. And appears a she-moose running.

GIANNA laughs, remembering the moose that day along the road: What was the animal running away from? Or was it running because it was dusk and the moose needed to hide for the night, I wonder?

GREGOR: Where do animals go when they die? We rarely encounter a carcass.

GIANNA: We did, one summer. Remember? The mountain sheep by the river.

GREGOR, turning off Gianna's headlamp: Must have been a recent death. Nature's cleaning crew had not found it yet.

PRELUDE TO A FALL

GIANNA: That same summer on one of our outings, I was traversing a narrow, exposed ledge. Many handholds, but you cannot trust the Rockies rock. Crumbly limestone. Portable handholds, the climbers call these rocks. As I moved along the ledge, I tested and retested each rock I grabbed before putting weight on them. Then, I made one move, and one hold stayed in my hand. That sudden release threw me off balance and the momentum caused my body to spin around. Now with my back to the rock wall, facing the void, I saw, really saw, myself falling. I screamed. A brief, strangulated scream. Pure reaction to the prelude to the fall.

Gregor had already traversed and from above, he called my name. The sound muffled as the rock face stood between us. Later, he told me his heart had jumped in his throat. Watching the void, he expected to see my body in flight before hitting the rocky slope below. The great shadow puppets of our years together dislocated before his eyes. Everything over in a flash. Then, he saw nothing. Heard nothing. Called my name again.

I was going down, except that, apart from being crumbly, limestone is also rough. So, my pack caught on a small outcrop of the uneven surface of the wall and that resistance against limestone was enough to stop my forward motion. I corrected my balance. Carefully turned back to face the wall. Resumed the traverse to where the ledge widened to safety.

Many long seconds later, he spotted the top of my helmet contouring the wall. I scrambled up toward him. He held me tight. That was a close call, I said.

BITTER BREW

Morning light. We crawl out of the tent at eight. Waiting for the pot to boil, we chew on stale bagels and cream cheese. Study the mountain in sunshine.

GREGOR: It's coming into shape again.

GIANNA: It kept me awake all night.

GREGOR: What kept you awake? The stage fright of the climb?

GIANNA: Climbers showing up today. Beating us to the climb.

GREGOR: Stop torturing yourself with things you can't change.

GIANNA: There will never be perfection to the days.

GREGOR: Brace yourself. The same story keeps repeating itself. We're caught in a causality loop.

GIANNA: Our personal causality loop?

GREGOR: There's no way out, Gia. None. No matter how swollen this part is or seized up that part becomes, we must keep in shape. Continue to climb.

GIANNA: The old couple doing the geriatric *assault* of mountains.

GREGOR: Worse yet. No longer able to recall, the old couple *assaulting* the same mountain over and over.

GIANNA: The old couple being assaulted by geriatric
　deterioration.

GREGOR: Take heart. The mountaineering industry will dream
　up walkers fitted with crampons.

GIANNA: And anti-gravity boots.

GREGOR: And fusion ice screws for arthritic fingers.

We pour the tea. Sip the brew.

GIANNA: We, annoying baby boomers, now dopey senile
　boomers.

GREGOR: The Whatever-Something gen can't wait for us to fall
　off the mountains, so they can have the mall to themselves.

We fill the pot with water again. The Assiniboine come back
to mind.

　A branch of the Sioux people, the Assiniboine hailed from
Lake of the Woods, but were displaced farther and farther
westward by the European conquest of North America. As we
will be displaced by the hordes demanding resorts and services.
More signs, the man from Maryland insisted. Along the way, the
Assiniboine tried to escape smallpox and, fleeing, they clashed
with other Natives. While we try to escape noisy machines and
helicopter tours. On the great prairies and until they reached the
mountains, the Assiniboine fought the tribes of the Blackfoot
Confederacy. We're fighting RVs and tour buses on winding
mountain roads. Meet the Invincible Indians. Conflicts, killings.
Eventually, the rivalry became less deadly in the guise of ritual
games. How far will we have to adapt?

　In our day and age, the Invincible Climbers wage rivalry
and contests over mountain faces, ridges and in couloirs.
Sometimes, their drive, ambition, fanaticism cause renewed
clashes. And mishaps. And they struggle against land itself. Even

with the new gizmos the mountaineering industry continuously invents, even then, the land resists those repeated assaults, and climbers fall. Though, each decade, climbers raise the bar a notch higher, putting ever more difficult routes where, previously, no human thought it possible for the law of gravity to be defied. How far can that go?

We pour more tea into our mugs. Watch the mountain dry itself in the sun.

When first climbed in 1903 by a W. Douglas and his *two* Swiss guides, the North Ridge of Mount Assiniboine was considered a challenge. No doubt was a challenge for Outram when, two years previously, he came down the same ridge, after summiting. Now, the mountain is climbed routinely dozens of times a year. Even in winter. And even in adverse conditions, you can always find Invincible Climbers willing to challenge, to defy, to *conquer*.

GREGOR: And we too must endure.

GIANNA: But the hordes...

GREGOR: You and your hordes!

GIANNA: We will run out of luck. Did you hear? The
    backcountry trails have reopened. And it's the weekend!
    They're coming, Greg! They're coming!

GREGOR: To avoid the crowds, we'll bushwhack. Climb at night.

GIANNA: No good. With night-vision goggles on the market, a
    nocturnal fad will develop. There'll be lineups.

Taking a liking to the mountains, the Assiniboine attacked the Kootenay, the true mountain dwellers, who must have objected to those upstarts from the east muscling in on their territory. In time, the Kootenay tolerated them and the Assiniboine stayed. Cooking their food with hot stones.

GREGOR: Until metal pots caught up with everybody.

GIANNA: And ever since, we've been scrubbing like mad.

GREGOR: Tomorrow, we get up and we climb. The mountain will
be in shape.

Another full day and one long night. Waiting. Mountaineering is
also about waiting. Anguish rising.

GIANNA: I hear voices.

GREGOR: It's only me mumbling.

Sipping tea in the falling quiet of morning. Will today be fine?
Will tomorrow be sweet? Sipping tea. Bitter brew.

CRIMSON NIGHT

We wake around midnight. Summer nights at this latitude are
never truly dark. We've been lying in our sleeping bags since
eight thirty. We must be rested for tomorrow's climb. Feeling
woozy sleepy. Falling into lightning-quick dreams. Hearing the
distant rumble of an avalanche.

Eyes closed. Silence broken. Something stepping on twigs.
High alert. We feel each other tensing up in our sleeping bags.
We try to relax. Grizzlies walk on silent paws. Eyes now wide
open, as if seeing helped to identify the source of the sound.

In so many of our deep conversations, we speculate that we
would take our life-altering disaster, whether an accident or
health failing, with eyes wide open, knowing too well it would
not prevent the catastrophic event from destroying who we
were. Gone, the full man/woman before the event. If the full
personality of the woman/man survived the catastrophe, who
can begin to imagine the cruelty of her life? his life? Day in, day
out, the long-distance walker immobilized. Day in, day out, the
climber paralyzed in a wheelchair.

A long time ago on stage in the Far East, when we were young and our old age was an impossibility, we performed old *Baucis and Philemon* in shadowgraphy and in a wig of white silk hair that came down to the floor.

Tonight, lying on our backs, zipped up in sleeping sheaths on the ground, faces a few inches from fragile textile, we are old Baucis and Philemon, without shadowgraphy, without wig of white hair. We wouldn't stand a chance should one of those silent paws take a swipe. And so tonight, we recall the ancient request of the old couple to the gods.

GREGOR: We have lived our years together in harmony.
GIANNA: Grant that we may die together.

Ears to the ground listening. Twigs breaking. The tent walls shaking. The gods entering our vestibule?

FEMALE VOICE: Howdy, folks. Sorry to startle you, but you must get up. I'm the warden. We're evacuating everybody at first light. It's a precautionary measure.
GREGOR and GIANNA: Fire?
WARDEN: On the other side of the pass. We don't think it'll reach the park. But we must evacuate anyway.

Grim thoughts tumble out of mind when urgency, perhaps that long-anticipated life-altering catastrophe hitting us, together, sooner than we think, jolts us into action. Yanks us out of what strange dreams, we forget.

WARDEN: You have time to take down your tent and pack your gear.

And we hear her walk away. The forest burning? Is that real? On the other side of the pass? How distant is that for a fast-burning fire?

We move. Unzipping sleeping bags. Slipping into pants. Lacing up boots. Grabbing small objects we had brought into the tent last night. Eyeglasses, headlamps, heart pills, water bottles, fleece caps. Unzipping tent door. Crawling out.

On the side of the pass invisible to us, we imagine a world aglow. Acrid smoke stinging eyes, choking lungs. High flames leaping into the starry sky, consuming wood at an astonishing rate, rushing upslope toward the pass. Nothing of the sort. Not even a red glow in the sky. All is quiet and it is later than we thought. Nearly three. We stuff the sleeping bags into their sacks. Empty the air out of the pads and roll them up. Fold the tarp. Take down the tent.

Rushing to retrieve the food bag from the metal cache. A fleeting thought as we stumble over the uneven ground. If we had attempted the mountain sooner, we would be high above in our world of snow and verglas. Would we still be alive to watch the inferno in the distance? Rushing back to the campsite.

We dump our gear into our packs. Shoulder packs, grab mountaineering axes. Hurry downhill toward the creek. Glance back, expecting the blaze now working its way over the pass. The speed of a wild fire can be astounding, terrifying. A lifetime of brain synapses destroyed in a matter of minutes. We pick up the pace. On our backs, the gear weighs heavily.

GIANNA: Should we dump ballast?
GREGOR: Are you crazy!

Stumbling over roots in eerie darkness backlit in pulsating reds and yellows, we imagine, we half-hike, half-jog on the snaking narrow trail circling the lake. The water, pristine and passive, a mirror for the stars. Somewhere, not that far, the blaze lights up the night. Mountains lighting up our lives.

We breathe hard, lungs tightening, and we trot. Trusting the tightness in our chests is lung- and not heart-related. With our packs on our backs and at night in this terrain, we can't run full tilt. Not anymore. In our hell-for-leather days, perhaps. Now, we settle for what the body can still do. If this night were then, we'd be flying across this meadow, finding the epic exhilarating, cutting across danger like cutting across a field of buttercups. There is no reason to rush. We relax our pace. But keep playing mental games. If we had had to flee and abandon the gear. The tent, tarp, sleeping bags and pads would be a brief torch of synthetic fibres, now melted and fused to the ground not unlike a puddle of human cells after the ultimate global annihilation.

Disconnected images downloading into our brains. These intrusions of the larger world are our firewall to keep us from losing our nerve. Not that we are in any real danger. But in the mountains, loss of nerve is loss of self.

We reach the lodge. Look back. Mount Assiniboine rises high above, rock no longer snow-plastered. Up there, calm and cold. Down here, havoc and heat one pass away. On the ground over there, ahead of a wall of flaming trees, panicked mice and hares, marmots and squirrels escaping. Bears and deer running shoulder to shoulder, not concerned which is friend, which is foe.

The lodge operators on the phone and their staff gathering guests are on full evac mode. Guests crowd around, silent and disciplined, awaiting instructions. A father clutching his two small children tells us that, a little farther away at the park cabin, the warden is working the radio. Since no rescue helicopters are available on account of the other wildfires burning in the two contiguous provinces, she is hard at work coordinating with headquarters. Commercial helicopters will fly from Canmore at first light. What if the conflagration jumps over the pass? And faster than expected? Still sheltering his children, the father also speculates about the logistics of their timely rescue. We are all brightly awake to this world.

GIANNA and GREGOR: How can we help?

THE OPERATORS, not mincing words: By not getting in the way. The guests are our responsibility. One thing you can do. The Naiset Cabins are mostly empty, except for a couple of hikers and two male climbers. We've already warned them to assemble here, but we don't see them yet. Could you...

GREGOR: Sure. But my wife and I will hike out.

THE OPERATORS, getting annoyed: We don't advise it. If you have an accident, we won't be able to send help.

GREGOR: We'll be all right.

It is clear our plan is not welcome, but we don't want to wait idle for hours. We look at Assiniboine denied us. At the very least, we'll give ourselves the consolation prize of a thirty-odd-kilometre nocturnal hike. Together in the mountains, always, feeding on the one's strength and resolve when the other's are waning.

GIANNA: All right. Let's do it.

We're all geared up, ready to hike out.

The operators suggest the safest way for us is via the Valley of the Rocks and Citadel Pass en route to Sunshine Village.

GIANNA: How will we hitch a ride from there to get back to our car in Canmore?

GREGOR: That's not important now.

No, it's not. We may even camp at Sunshine. We have the gear, we have food. And when rested, why not hike all the way to Canmore? It's not as if we had never hiked long distance before.

First though, we must check on the occupants of the Naiset Cabins. A short distance from the lodge at the primitive huts, we flash our headlamps into darkness. Empty. In one cabin, a man and a woman are gathering their gear. We briefly discuss with them the route we will take. Not eager either to wait for a helicopter, the hikers will also go via Citadel Pass. They remind us of us thirty years ago, in our prime.

GREGOR: You should inform the lodge operators or the warden of your decision. They won't like it, but they should know.

We enter more cabins. Darkness. Emptiness. We open the last door. Shine our lights on two guys in bunk beds. Bleary-eyed, they raise themselves up on their elbows.

CLIMBER ONE: What the fuck! Turn off those goddam lights!
CLIMBER TWO: Yeah, man. What's this? The third degree?
GREGOR: Guys, get up.
CLIMBER ONE: Get up? We just got to bed.
CLIMBER TWO: Yeah, man. We need our beauty sleep.
GREGOR: We are being evacuated. You were told. You must leave now.
CLIMBER ONE: Leave? We were here first.
CLIMBER TWO: Yeah, man. Go get your own cabin.
GREGOR: Okay, pals. You want to burn to a crisp? Suit yourselves.
CLIMBER ONE: And close the door. Who's that old geezer ordering us around?

CLIMBER TWO: Yeah, man. Tourists! A blister and they
whimper for a rescue.

GIANNA: They're pretty cocky. But we're not exactly playing by
the rules either.

GREGOR: What's our duty now? Drag those bozos out and force-
march them to the helipad? And if they resist? Engage them
in a fist fight, à la crazy-Brit climbers circa 1970s brawling in
the pubs? Demolishing the cabin in the process?

GIANNA: Itching for a good old-fashioned fight, Greggy? They're
big boys.

We leave the door open, should the fire appear over the pass and
shine its red eye at the Invincible Climbers. Then, let them make
their own calculations.

Our headlamps light the dark trail ahead. Into the silence of
the night, without slowing down our pace, we quip to keep up
the rhythm.

GREGOR: Those two climbers. We should have attacked them.

GIANNA: Boiled water in a bison skin and gotten out the pliers.

GREGOR: Made them bite the bullet.

GIANNA: Must settle for a piton. Bullets are forbidden in a park.

GREGOR: Aye. Is it possible to extract the complacency of
toughness, that peculiar form of ego common to Invincible
Climbers, without pulling half the patient's brain out with it,
thus killing both the parasite and the host?

GIANNA: Or is complacency of toughness something that must
fall off on its own in due course?

GREGOR: That is, if invincibility itself doesn't first kill its bearer.

GIANNA: We were that cocky once. We were.

For the last time, and before the hilly landmass hides it from us, we turn around to glance at Mount Assiniboine. What is happening to those two climbers in their cabin? Wrapped in invincibility, tomorrow when they climb the mountain, will they be consumed in the fire of their own ritual game? As we know too well, in the mountains, everything has always been a matter of calculated risk. And we each calculate our personal invincibility by a slightly different set of variables, assigning to each his equation of limits. As have done the Assiniboine and Kootenay, Blood and Peigan and Blackfoot, and all the White upstarts, and us in this crazy mix, who have clung to rock.

Hiking away from our crimson night, we can't help wondering how our own egos will manage to survive this farewell to love.

VALLEY OF THE ROCKS

And now in the Valley of the Rocks, we anticipate our last day out.

Crimson pulsating behind our eyelids. Who will be the first? Which one of us will watch the other jump over the Big Void? The other one's corpse. At the bottom of a cliff. Recovered from a frigid river. Accident? Or an act of will? Or inert on his/her unchosen narrow hospital bed, taken by surprise by the catastrophic falling-apart of the body, and catching her/his last breath? A prisoner of the commonplace. He/she who never felt at ease within the confinement of walls. Will the one departing have time or the ability to write a farewell note to the one lingering?

"We ask that I should not live to see her tomb, nor she survive to bury me in mine." Those are not our words. Baucis and Philemon, old love drawn in hand shadows. Played out long ago on a faraway stage.

Our farewell note to love will only require three words. Three words carefully written before one of us falls over the edge.

Dumping ballast. What do people expect those three words to be? I love you. Of course, but. As if that were news to us. Still, when nothing more can be said, when what needs to be said is infinite, people cling to *those* three words. I love you.

The one abandoned, now alone with the absence of the one gone. Left, not with the three expected words, but with three words of far greater significance. Three words that say everything to us. You understand me.

And the one left behind whispers: I do. Throat constricted, tears streaming, lying down alongside the one departed. Hugging the body close. As we did so often, both of us alive, alive, after a particularly trying day in the mountains. "That was a close call." And now, those last three words. You understand me. Lips whispering: I do.

The one left behind speaks:

> I understand that your great crimson night had not chased you
> off yourself.
> I understand that the full you was still intact, but trapped in
> the terminally ill body shell.
> I understand that you waited until you could exit the long
> way out.
> I understand that this had to be done right the first time.
> I understand that you still dreamed robust dreams. And in the
> cruelty of your endless waking hours, you visualized climbs
> yet to come. The faster we lose it, the faster we will lose it.

Reconstructing our laughter and our deep conversations. Reaffirming our perfect understanding, even when, at times, we begged to differ. Bracing against the dread of one leaving the other. The survivor's grief and the departing one causing acute pain.

> *I understand that, the whole mountain life being taken away*
> *from us by the coming hordes, you took the summit down*
> *into the river with you.*
> *I understand that I must not hate your ego, Invincible Climber,*
> *but must celebrate this event, which you set in motion to*
> *restore your freedom of movement, of speech, of thought.*
> *Your fierce avoidance of the commonplace.*
> *I understand that you are now free to free climb past your age*
> *and the ages.*
> *I understand that this farewell to love is a climbing accident of*
> *another kind.*

As the one left behind hugs the departed one close, he/she must do this one last act before letting go of the belay. And so, on this crimson night, let us tell each other everything, as we always have.

We will reach the summit of Assiniboine via the North Ridge in brilliant sunshine. First though, we will revisit together our long wondrous climb that began decades earlier, in another place, in another time.

And shivering in the cold night, we prepare to leave the Valley of the Rocks in silence.

CLOSING TIME

But despite the sharp air, we cannot bring ourselves to resume the hike down.

GREGOR: We did not invest enough in the mountains.
GIANNA: We could have gone higher, deeper, farther.
GREGOR, throwing a stone into the darkness of distance:
  Hindsight, Gianna. End-of-life regrets. Let's not go there.

We agree. Tonight, keenly fearing the confinement of walls.

So, we set our packs on the ground. Watch the stars, identifying constellations. We exchange thoughts about the universe. Time and infinity; lives reaching their bounds at the speed of light. Destiny; and the density of destiny. The continuous string of our lives so easily snapped. Trifles of that nature. We imprint on our minds Mount Assiniboine the way we saw it tonight, the way we will never see it again. Mount Assiniboine changing its rocky aspects in the various light exposures of day fading into night. The North Ridge, its sharp edge blurring in the darkening of evening. Higher up, the summit imagined. With its cornice of old, old snow.

So, we keep watch. Listen to the quiet. In silence, solitude, stillness.

In this simple manner, we stay linked, sitting side by side on the hard ground as if we were above and beyond our finality.

Acknowledgements

IT HAS BECOME an established practice to acknowledge the individuals in the writer's entourage who have contributed to the words you have read or are about to read. Long before I became a writer, I had no doubt that the creative works I was reading were the sole responsibility of the authors who penned them. Perhaps there are still such writers; perhaps they never existed.

It is my turn to acknowledge those who helped shape this book. We may be alone in our writing room, day in, day out, with our language(s), characters, stories, imagination, but the contribution of others keeps us from deluding ourselves.

To that effect, I wish to thank Tom Back, Adrian Michael Kelly, and Anne Sorbie, who read the stories with a sharp eye and an open mind.

My special thanks go to my editor, Maya Fowler, whom I had never met before we embarked on this collaboration, but with whom our exchanges about writing and languages were as if we had known each other for years. Her contribution has been invaluable.

I also wish to thank the entire team at the University of Alberta Press, especially Peter Midgley for opening the door to my work and Alan Brownoff for having the wisdom to forgo putting a mountain on the cover.

And to you, dear readers, whether you are rising abruptly or walking gently through these stories, my wish is that you don't fall and hit the deck, but enjoy the climb as much as I have, whether on rock or with words.

In "Assiniboine Crossroads," the Baucis and Philemon quote is from Ovid's *Metamorphoses*, translated by Charles Martin (New York: W.W. Norton & Company, 2004) and cited in Alice Major's *Memory's Daughter* (Edmonton: University of Alberta Press, 2010).

"Nuit Blanche with Gendarme" is an English adaptation of one of the stories in my French collection, *Outsiders* (Montréal: Lévesque éditeur, 2013). Used by permission.

"Nepal High" is an adaptation of one of the chapters in my French novel, *Rumeurs de la Haute Maison*, (Montréal: Québec Amérique, 1987).

Other Titles from The University of Alberta Press

YOU HAVEN'T CHANGED A BIT
Stories
ASTRID BLODGETT
184 pages
Robert Kroetsch Series
978-0-88864-644-6 | $19.95 paper
978-0-88864-712-2 | $15.99 EPUB
978-0-88864-713-9 | $15.99 Kindle
978-0-88864-809-9 | $15.99 PDF
Literature / Short Stories

RUDY WIEBE
Collected Stories, 1955–2010
RUDY WIEBE
THOMAS WHARTON, *Introduction*
552 pages | Critical introduction, appendices, selected
bibliography
A volume in cuRRents, a Canadian Literature Series
978-0-88864-540-1 | $39.95 paper
Literature / Short Stories

A MINOR PLANET FOR YOU
and Other Stories
LESLIE GREENTREE
208 pages
A volume in cuRRents, a Canadian Literature Series
978-0-88864-465-7 | $24.95 paper
978-0-88864-854-9 | $19.99 PDF
Literature / Short Stories